HOUSE OF DADS

A Hillary Broome Novel

June Gillam

Also by June Gillam

Creating Juicy Tales
So Sweet Against Your Teeth
House of Cuts

Published by Gorilla Girl Ink, USA
ISBN 978-0-9858838-2-9

November 2005

ONE

Violet

I WAITED in front of the church for Teddy, little dreaming it would be the last time my brother was ever late. For anything.

He mounted the granite steps, his camel hair coat buttoned against the November chill, in no hurry on this gloomy Saturday we were to bury our father. Teddy flashed his brilliant smile, a gleaming contrast against the darkness of the day. He knew everything and everyone would wait for him.

"Come on," I hissed and pulled open the door into Holy Family's dim foyer. "It was supposed to start at three!"

"I had a couple deals cooking," Teddy said.

Deals cooking. His way of cooking, so different from mine. I'd just come from helping with the reception meal. I led him in the direction of the crowded sanctuary. The front doors of the church opened and closed behind us, admitting a frigid wind along with a couple of bankers, part of Dad's good-ol'-boy circle. They rushed past us, nodding respects to my twin brother and patting me on the shoulder.

Mournful notes of "Day of Wrath" poured from the organ to further darken my mood. Our workaholic father had collapsed last week, his high-pressure lifestyle causing a massive heart attack. How would his death affect our family business? Will I still be kept shut away in the accounting department, a dainty mouse forever nibbling at crumbs?

Teddy stood in the foyer, his face fresh with vigor, a man on his way up in the world. I grabbed his arm and pulled him down a narrow side hallway. The bereaved family always sat in a recessed space behind a sheer curtain in the crossbar of the sanctuary, laid out in a traditional floor plan. Lodi's Holy Family Church was just over a century old, a mix of domed and arched spaces.

Cousin Hillary sat with some man I didn't know in the last row of the family alcove. I wondered about her. She was the only child of Uncle Gerald, who'd ignored our family business in favor of becoming a newspaperman. She was a reporter, too. The only other thing I knew about her was that her mother had run off when Hillary was young.

Now that I thought of it, it wouldn't have been so bad if our mother had left—instead of tearing me down, year after year. There she sat, in the front row of the alcove, a steely figure draped in black lace. As if psychic, she turned to scowl at me, her dark eyes narrow, the corners of her thin lips pressed tight.

I looked away and tugged at the soft golden wool of Teddy's sleeve to get him to hurry, but he stopped at an antique coat tree standing in a corner.

"Come on!" I shoved my fists deep into the pockets of my black skirt. I wished I'd had time to stop in the powder room to check my supplies. The damn curse always came at the worst time. Each period since my marriage was another bloody reminder I was not yet pregnant with a chance for a son, who could inherit controlling interest in the family business.

Only after his coat hung to his satisfaction did Teddy take a seat in the space reserved for us and our mother, aunties, and cousins—all female. Teddy was now the only male left in the family.

Thank God, Teddy and I were at the opposite end from Mother, sitting next to Aunt Helena. Mother held her chin up, eyes dry as the witchy queen's in a fairy tale.

The funeral began.

Father Dale took a somber tone. "We are here to honor Robert Broome, pillar of our community." The priest shot a piercing stare over at the open casket. His gaze drew everyone's attention to Dad's profile, outlined against the satin lining of the lid. Even now, he seemed to radiate a fierce energy, bringing the heat of a California sun into this winter day.

With a sickening lurch in my belly, I noticed how much Dad looked like Grandad ten years ago. Dad's hair was black, though, instead of bright red like Grandad's and Teddy's. Black Irish, Dad was called, same as me. I pressed my hand to my abdomen and rubbed in small circles to soothe my cramps. I needed one of my pain capsules but they were at home. Rolling my shoulders to ease the tension, I looked at Teddy.

Coolly, he slid his hand into his breast pocket and pulled out a business card case engraved with his initials below the Broome Construction BC logo. That case was a gift on our thirtieth birthday while my present was another "collector's" doll. My cheeks burned with the memory.

While Father Dale described God's many mansions, Teddy jotted notes on the backs of several business cards. Voice soaring, the priest enthused over Dad's new life with Jesus, detailing its streets-of-gold pleasures. "And now, Robert's son will say a few words."

Teddy parted the sheer curtain screening off the alcove, stepped up to the pulpit, and looked out over the crowd. For the first time, it hit me that his fiancée Bridget wasn't here. How could she be missing this important occasion? I was loath for him to marry anyone, though, and start cranking out a line of boy babies to keep me out of my rightful place in Broome Construction.

Teddy began. "When the Lord took my grandfather, Dad stepped up to fill his shoes, and he tried to ready me for the rugged world of business." My brother was starting to sound like our father, speaking with a lilt that charmed friends and transformed enemies. Teddy's face shone as he recounted Grandad's immigration from Ireland and his hard-won success as an American housing developer. A beam of sunlight broke through the clouds and shot through a stained glass window. It played across Teddy's square-jawed face, highlighting his bright blue eyes. Finally, Teddy tucked his notes into his breast pocket and sat down.

The priest began. "Our Father . . ."

I couldn't keep focused on the prayer. Teddy was starting to run the business, now that Dad was gone. My request for more responsibilities had never been taken seriously. It was so unfair. I was the builder and Teddy the ballplayer. Even back in kindergarten, I wanted to build. I was the one to stack up those hollow wooden blocks, big as squared-off bedroom pillows. I'd stack them high as I could reach and fasten them in place. The other girls would play house in them.

The priest went on. "Give us this day . . ."

Every summer day from sixth grade on, I'd worked at Broome Construction, but always in the office under Mom's glaring eye. Dad tried to get Teddy out to the warehouse and shops, but Teddy would beg off to go play baseball. Each time I complained and said I wanted to work in the shop, Mother came up with a new job she called "appropriate" for a young lady. She taught me how to make certain the bathroom was clean, the books balanced each month, and the Folgers turned out perfect in her electric percolator.

For years, a wordless prayer beat through my blood, a prayer that athletic and handsome Teddy would become a rich and famous professional baseball player, turn down the business, and somehow, I would get to carry it on.

That dream was still alive. Even though married to my wonderful Buddy, I kept and treasured my maiden name: Violet Broome. As close to the action as I was allowed to get was to be chief accountant at BC.

The priest droned on to the end of the prayer: "For thine is the kingdom, and the power . . ."

The power.

Now Teddy was the head of Broome Construction. I was next in line after my brother even though I was the oldest twin by six minutes.

A devil thought slipped into my mind: *What if something happens to Teddy.*

Shocked, I clamped off that idea and stared through the alcove's sheer curtain to study the intricate carvings of saints clustered around the base of Father Dale's pulpit. Martyred St. Perpetua caught my attention. She was wearing a dark red gown, bringing to mind the color of paprika.

Paprika. Joanna and I had bought a big package of it after that San Francisco chef gave us his recipe. "Paprika," he'd said, "put in plenty."

Father Dale brought the service to an end. He invited guests to mingle in the parish hall for a meal to follow shortly after the private burial. Teddy rose and walked down to take Mother by her gloved hands. She smiled up at him, her face glowing, and stood to embrace him. Her golden boy.

I slipped out and headed for the powder room to change my wadding. The stores might call it feminine hygiene products, but I liked to call it wadding, after a word I'd heard one of Dad's hunting buddies use. Wadding. I felt like a gun myself, full of wadding keeping my bullets inside.

TWO

Hillary

WIND GUSTED against Hillary's back as she followed her family out toward the limousine. Fighting the chill air, Hillary pulled her trench coat collar tight against her neck. She stepped up into the dark cave of the limo. Her cousin Ted and his mother Maggie already sat side by side, back at the rear. Hillary almost tripped over Violet, sitting behind the driver's seat, as far from her mother and brother as possible.

Hillary motioned her fiancé Ed to follow her in. They centered themselves on the bench seats across from the door, while behind them came cousin Joanna and her husband to sit on the opposite side.

Before the funeral, Hillary had not spoken with any of them. She'd sat behind the rose-colored curtain, one of them but feeling like an outsider. It hadn't bothered her while her father was alive. His booming presence was all the family she'd needed. But since his sudden death last May, a need to reach out to them was growing inside her.

She was grateful when Joanna came up after the service and insisted she join them for the burial, pointing out that she was the cousin next line after Ted, Violet, and Joanna herself. Hillary wondered about the younger girl cousins, but they didn't seem to count.

Hillary glanced toward the back of the limo. Ted's arm rested around his mother's shoulder as he murmured in her ear. Maggie sat stony-faced, looking as frozen as a Madonna sculpture in a cemetery. *Mothers. What does my mother look like now?* Hillary squeezed her eyes shut tight, holding back tears.

She sat motionless in the quiet shrouding the family as they set out on Robert Broome's short and final ride. Hillary wondered if it was the right time to introduce Ed and decided against it. She glanced at Violet, whose eyes were closed. Last year Violet had married a doctor named Buddy. Kind of sweet to have a buddy for a husband, Hillary remembered thinking when she'd heard about it from her father.

They hadn't been invited to the wedding, and her father acted like he didn't care. She wished she'd asked more about his family while he was still alive. His will had directed no funeral service, so there had been no chance for her to feel consolation from these people last spring. *If they are the consoling sort.*

The silence was unnerving. Hillary cleared her throat. When Violet turned and opened her eyes, Hillary asked, "Where's Buddy?"

"An emergency patient," Violet muttered, looking down at her hands, clenched in her lap. "Asthma attack." She leaned forward to tug at the hem of her wool coat just as her stomach growled with a gurgle. She pressed her hand to her belly and hunched forward.

Hillary didn't know what else to say. She hadn't spent much time with these relatives. Over the past decade or so, she'd been busy working up in Sacramento, then out to New York's Colombia for her master's. None of the Broome family ever paid attention to her, either— Grandad Patrick had ostracized Hillary's father years ago for his lack of interest in the construction business.

But now that she felt orphaned by her father's death, and didn't know if her mother was even still among the living, a new and deep loneliness was creeping into her. She found herself taking time to watch families as she stood in line at the grocery store.

Being asked to go along for this brief service at the graveside was another chance to observe the Broomes. *Observe.* Being a reporter had kept her so distant from people. She leaned her head against Ed's shoulder and closed her eyes. *How does he feel about family?*

The limo pulled up behind the hearse and parked at a curb fifty feet from a white canopy set up to shelter the newly dug grave. Men in dark suits were carrying floral arrangements from the hearse to lay them on an Astro-turf-covered mound.

The Broome family climbed out of the limo and made their way up the slight incline.

A man rushed past them, waving a picket sign high in the air and running toward the gravesite. On his sign were scrawled thick black initials, BC, inside a circle with a diagonal line slashed through it.

Ted bellowed out, "Hey! Get the hell away from here, you ghoul!" The man backed off. Ted took his mother by the arm and hurried her along to a folding chair under the canopy, facing away from where the silent picketer paced back and forth, his sign bobbing.

Hillary frowned at Ed. "Holy Mary!" She nodded at the man, wearing a gray hooded sweatsuit. "I saw him in church and wondered about how he was dressed," she said, "but I didn't see any sign. Isn't there some kind of law against harassment at a funeral?"

Ed looked at her, lips pressed tight and brow furrowed. He shook his head. "Free speech."

Hillary spotted a couple security men keeping an eye on the picketer. "He better not show up at the reception," she said, wondering what his story was. She would have to write it up for *The Acorn*, the weekly paper she worked at. But she was part of this Broome family and could be losing her objectivity—she was supposed to just report the news, not be part of it.

Pallbearers carried the casket from the hearse and positioned it on a platform set out over the open grave. White roses in the arrangement atop the casket fluttered in the light wind. Hillary watched Violet march around to the far side of the casket, directly opposite from her mother and brother. Hillary followed Violet, feeling a visceral need to balance opposing sides, as if she were at a high school basketball game. Other mourners gathered, a few glancing at the threatening gray clouds above.

Hillary noticed a shapely blonde in a belted red raincoat stride over to Ted's side. The woman reached out to tug on his coat sleeve but spoke so quietly Hillary couldn't make out what she said. Ted yanked his arm away as if her red-tipped fingers were poison. He glared at her and muttered out of the side of his mouth, then turned toward his mother and nodded for them to sit down. Frowning, the blonde moved a few yards away, where she stood with her lips pursed.

Father Dale offered a series of short prayers. "Dust though art…" Dust. Hillary's father's ashes had been more like gravel than dust. He had prepaid to be cremated and scattered in San Francisco Bay. Hillary had followed his wishes. Now tears streamed down her cheeks. Ed handed her his big white handkerchief.

The priest's final words were in Latin. She'd been too numb to say any kind prayers as she poured her father's ashes out into the cold water of the bay. She wiped her cheeks and cleared her throat.

Ted stood and laid his palm at the head of his father's casket for a moment, then stepped back and made the sign of the cross on himself. He nodded to his mother, who did the same, and the two of them turned and walked toward the waiting limo.

Hillary's reporter's instincts quickened when a couple of men in dark suits rushed to Ted's side, their arms extended to shake hands. Ted turned away and strode past them without a glance, leading his mother to the open door of the limousine. The two men exchanged frowns. The younger one shrugged his well-tailored shoulders.

Hillary wondered who they were and what caused Ted's hostile reaction to them. It might be some grim reception, she thought. *Doesn't anyone like anyone else around here?*

THREE

Violet

I GOT OUT OF THE LIMO, glad to escape Mother's frosty face, and hurried into the church kitchen. Aunt Helena, mother to Joanna and her five sisters, had beat me back there. She stood and peered into the restaurant-sized kettle of goulash Joanna and I'd started that morning. Aunt Helena looked at me, her salt-and-pepper eyebrows dovetailed into a question.

"It's a new recipe," I said. "Joanna and I discovered it last month." I smiled at her and slipped my apron on, smoothing it over my stomach. "With all the housing developments bringing in so many people, Joanna's going to open a European cafe downtown. Did you know?"

"Oh, my!" Aunt Helena frowned. "Our goulash wasn't good enough for Jojo?"

"Not at all! We love that hamburger-and-macaroni dish you taught us to make." I got an industrial-sized spoon down from one of the metal racks fastened to the pale green wall. "It's just that the new homeowners moving here from the Bay Area have more sophisticated tastes."

"Smells spicy, at least, after that long dull service." She walked over to help Great Aunt Sophie, who was starting to cut up desserts. The kitchen and parish hall were parallel with the main church and working with food here seemed kind of sacred in its own way. The half dozen ladies on the funeral committee felt so, judging by their serene faces as they helped us get ready.

I stirred the fragrant and meaty goulash. Early that morning, I'd helped Joanna brown the cubed and floured pork, along with pounds of thin-sliced onions. Then it was left to simmer for hours. It tasted divine when we first discovered it in San Francisco's Little Prague Café. The chef was generous enough to give us his recipe but insisted we had to find authentic paprika. We were shocked to see it called for only four other ingredients. We had tried a small batch last week and received big thumbs-up from our husbands. Joanna's Milan said it reminded him of the Czech cooking his mom did when he was a kid.

The mingled flavors, dark red color, and meaty texture seemed the perfect main dish for this frigid winter day. With plenty of hot crusty bread and tossed salad on the side, I felt sure it would please these people gathered to honor my father. Not to mention the sweets the aunties were contributing.

I looked over to check on desserts. Great Aunt Sophie—a spry eighty-five—waved a silver knife over her specialty, a coffee-colored cake towering six inches high on its crystal cake plate. "When your Uncle Johnny was little, his favorite was this hazelnut cake," she sang out in my direction. "He could eat a quarter of it himself. I baked it up in his memory. Too many of our men dying off." She plunged the knifepoint into the cake's center and drew the handle down with vigor, as if she were working a paper cutter. She began slicing portions while Aunt Helena held small plates to take each slice. The church still used sturdy china dishes and stainless flatware, even though it was more work than paper and plastic. Cooking and serving men was what the women in this church were good at, especially the women in our family.

"I want that recipe, Aunt Sophie." I smiled at her, wondering if she knew Joanna was starting a Euro-Cuisine restaurant. Some of Sophie's elegant recipes might be hot sellers in our Central Valley market, more upscale by the month as Broome Construction and other housing developments had started popping up like mushrooms after rain during the past few years. The money was pouring in. Our BC profits were swelling.

A blast of heat from a massive oven door yanked my attention back to the kitchen. Hands wrapped in tea towels, Aunt Mary pulled out a rack of *kolach,* filled with poppy seed paste. This was Teddy's favorite pastry from childhood, and he could eat a dozen of the little goodies with no trouble.

Joanna supervised her younger sisters as they transferred food into serving dishes and started carrying it out to the sideboards in the parish hall. I ladled goulash into a huge serving bowl that young Millie was holding with both arms. "Where's the corn and macaroni?" she wailed. "That's my favorite part!"

Feeling guilty, I explained how far off the mark our family recipe had been, telling her how Joanna and I had discovered authentic Czech goulash while researching for her new restaurant.

Hearing her name, Joanna approached the stove and stuck a spoon into the steaming meaty dish. She polished off a bite and grinned at me. "Good job, Violet." She gave a thumbs-up. "Plenty of that new paprika from the San Francisco shop." She took another spoonful, swallowed, and crowed, "You've got to come into the restaurant business with me, Vi, since Teddy's the big cheese standing alone now at BC." She threw me an evil grin. She thought she was so smart with her MBA. Not everyone knew about her visits to psychic readers like I did, though.

I ignored her and lifted the heavy bowl from Millie's arms, hefted it into a secure position, and backed out the swinging double doors into the parish hall, curious to see what reaction people would have to our new recipe. I set the bowl on the long sideboard we would serve up plates from soon. None of the aunties liked using buffet lines and since there were so many helping out, we could serve each person tableside. The wine, water, and lemonade carafes were out already, with plenty of breadsticks to crunch on. The antipasto plates were almost empty. I had to get more of those started. The room buzzed with people enjoying themselves, all here to pay respects to my father.

Wish I felt more like honoring him myself. He'd never given me a chance to show what I was capable of. But this was the twenty-first century. *My brother knows women are just as competent as men.* My twin, Teddy. All my dreams of being a builder now hinged on him.

FOUR

Hillary

HILLARY PEEKED into the church kitchen, looking for Joanna. One of the aunties was bent over the center island, placing celery and carrot sticks, olives and sliced salami onto china plates, so focused she didn't even look up. Hillary backed out and reminded herself she didn't need Joanna's invitation to take her place among the Broomes.

Hillary took hold of Ed's elbow. "Let's get a seat up in front." She headed for a couple of spots left open at a table reserved for family.

Ed filled their glasses from one of the water carafes while she took a couple long thin breadsticks from the

nearest container and passed one to him. He was unusu-
ally quiet today. Maybe funerals brought memories of
sad times. She wished there'd been some kind of service
for her father. She wondered who Ed had lost. She'd
fallen for the long, lean detective when she'd worked
with him last month on those awful murders at the superstore. But there was so much they didn't know about
each other yet.

She nodded in Ted's direction as he pushed his chair
back and stood, holding a glass of red wine and a spoon.
He looked out over the crowd. Hillary turned to observe
those assembled, doing a quick assessment for the brief
story she planned to write up later for the paper. She es-
timated a couple hundred had stayed on after the service
and assumed there was a fairly even mix of friends and
folks from the business community Robert had been so
much a part of.

Ted tapped his spoon several times against the glass.
In seconds the chatter in the room quieted. Hillary realized a natural authority flowed from this cousin she
barely knew.

"On behalf of our family, thank you for coming to
pay your respects," Ted began. "My mother sends her
apologies. She wanted to stay but Dr. Sloan sent her
home to rest." He cleared his throat and readjusted the
knot of his tie. "In case you're wondering about my fiancée, Bridget, she's in Ireland on what she called a pre-
wedding retreat. Getting away from both her father and
me—East and West Coast developers." There was an un-
dercurrent of laughter in the room, but Hillary thought

Ted's was louder than seemed warranted. What was up with him and his fiancée?

At a nearby table, Hillary spotted the woman Ted had wrested himself away from at the cemetery. She was glaring up at the ceiling, lips pursed tight. Suddenly she lifted her glass of wine and drained it.

"Who is that blonde?" Hillary mouthed to Ed, nodding in her direction. He took a quick look, shrugged, and turned back to focus on Ted, who continued his remarks.

Ted glanced down at a man seated at his side. "But here with me is my pal Zack. Always hoped I would end up in the baseball majors, but instead he made it to the bigs. And not just any team, but the Sox! Thanks for being here, buddy." Ted gave a couple hearty slaps on the back of a slim and fit fellow grinning up at him.

Ed nodded in recognition. Hillary also had heard of this Boston Red Sox pitcher, from her time out on the East Coast last year.

Ted glanced at the man seated at his other side. "My cousin-in-law, too," Ted grinned at Joanna's husband, Milan. "He's here. Not to focus on business today, but he's the financial wizard of Broome Construction, bringing some new contacts on board to keep us healthy now that Dad's no longer here to captain the ship." Ted shot a friendly punch to Milan's arm.

Hillary looked around the room for Violet, wondering how she would react. Wasn't Violet in the financial part of the company? The accountant or something? Hillary felt bad there was so much family business she was in the dark about. She looked forward to the reading of Robert's will. She could learn a lot there.

Ted's rich baritone carried on, inviting eulogies. "If anyone wants to speak now about their memories, please." He waved a hand in the air and sat down.

A young woman rose, holding her baby secure on her hip, and bubbled on about how grateful she was for Robert creating beautiful neighborhoods where before there had been just acres of swampy Delta sloughs. A middle-aged man stood and shared how he'd fled from the San Francisco Bay Area to find a better-priced home inland. Several others shared the impact Robert Broome had had on them. For the first time, Hillary felt proud of this little-known aspect of her family.

Then a man wearing a dark suit and striped tie stood and cleared his throat. Hillary recognized him as one of the pair who got the brush-off from Ted at the cemetery. "We at Mortenson Mortgage appreciate how generous Robert was sharing his knowledge and experience, lifting up so many in these good times we find ourselves blessed—"

Ted stood quickly, frowned and banged his spoon against his glass again, fast and hard. "Thank you, all of you. And now it's time to enjoy the meal put together by the talented ladies in the Broome family, who've been working their magic in the kitchen. Please, everyone," he raised his wine glass high, "as Grandad Patrick used to say--'Sláinte!'"

It sounded like 'slawn-cha' to Hillary as she joined in repeating the toast. She'd have to find out what it meant. Probably something like "to your health."

Ted nodded at Violet standing in the kitchen door-way. She and Joanna supervised as the young cousins and church ladies dished up food. Violet carried over a plate-ful and set it down at Ted's place. He gave her a squeeze around the waist, then started forking goulash into his mouth.

Hillary was interested in their relationship. They'd kept their distance at the cemetery, but sister and brother seemed friendly now. Was it because their mother was no longer nearby?

One of the cousins set a plate in front of Ed and one for Hillary. She couldn't tell these girls apart yet and wanted to make time to get their names put together with faces. Each plate contained goulash, tossed green salad, and warm buttered bread. Hillary noticed the macaroni and cheese substitute for goulash, green beans instead of salad, for the children. She recalled the creamy goodness of her father's mac and cheese. The comfort. An ache fell over her, part missing him and part an ache to hold a child of her own. She looked at Ed—how did he feel about having kids? In the short time since they'd met, that hadn't come up. Yet. She'd have to be the one to broach the subject.

Quiet minutes passed with murmurs of appreciation for the food. Hillary was just about to begin introducing Ed to nearby family members when she noticed a balding man wearing wire-rimmed glasses enter the hall. He strode toward Violet, standing near the kitchen. As she spotted him, Violet's pale face broke into a grin, and she leaned forward to reach out for a big hug.

Reaching to give Ed's hand a squeeze, she tipped her head in their direction. "There's cousin Vi's new husband. He's a doctor. Name of Buddy."

Ed looked over at them and leaned close to murmur in her ear, "When are we going down the aisle?" She hadn't let herself set a date. Yet. He gave her a couple kisses on the neck and nibbled her earlobe.

Hillary hoped no one would notice her blushing. That was the worst part about being a redhead. Her head was spinning, wondering what kind of wedding would be best. She distrusted big church affairs like the one that failed to keep her parents together, but she yearned to belong to Ed. And soon, before the years ran out on a chance to have her own family. Their family.

* * *

Within a half hour, the desserts—semi-sweet kolach, hazelnut cake, and vanilla ice cream—were served. Hillary recalled the crunchy poppy seeds in the kolach from the few times her father had taken her to a holiday gathering. She'd loved discovering one or two poppy seeds hiding in her teeth hours after she got home. Later in life she learned most people hated that, and it underscored how odd she was, how much she didn't belong. She turned to tell Ed this memory, confident he would understand, but out of nowhere, a ruckus arose at the doors to the parking lot.

A man burst into the hall, holding a picket sign aloft

in one hand. It was the same man from the cemetery. He jogged left, running around the room's perimeter, shouting. Hillary couldn't make out what he was yelling. He came to a sudden stop in front of Ted and raised his placard high, chanting "BC, BC– clean up your act! Mold kills—and that's a fact!" His words were clear now—and printed in bold black marker on both sides of his sign.

Ed stood, hand on hip over his concealed Glock, always prepared for danger. She wished she'd brought along her camera.

Clad in gray sweats and wearing black gloves, the man raised his other hand to brandish a small bullhorn. He put it to his lips and repeated his rhyme of protest, blasting loud as an announcer at a football game.

Chaos broke out. A baby began bawling and little kids jumped up with wide eyes, excited, and hopping from one foot to the other before their parents pulled them back into their chairs.

Still chewing, Ted rose and faced the man.

"Get out! You son of a bitch!" Ted bellowed, stabbing his fork toward the accuser who darted side to side, parrying Ted's thrusts. The man laughed in Ted's face, twisting the placard so both sides could be seen.

Bedlam reigned. Parents lifted crying toddlers into their arms, as older kids ran up to the front of the room. Ed was on his phone as he moved nearer the interloper.

"I told you to—" Ted clutched at his throat and grunted. He pitched forward toward his accuser, who dropped his bullhorn and backed away toward the doors he'd come in from. As he vanished, Ted collapsed onto the parish hall floor.

Hillary didn't know what to do. Ed rushed to grab the bullhorn. "Stay in your seats, everyone!" He moved around the room repeating directions to calm the crowd.

Ted thrashed from side to side on the floor, gasping and tugging at his necktie. Hillary wished she knew how to do the Heimlich or even how to recognize if it was needed. She felt relieved as Buddy rushed over to kneel at Ted's side.

"Are you choking?" Buddy yelled. Ted lifted his head and growled "Not," then coughed and slumped back wordless, limp on the floor.

Buddy loosened Ted's tie and swept a finger through his mouth, bent his cheek to Ted's lips, then began CPR.

Hillary felt time stop.

Paramedics arrived within minutes. Buddy stood to make room for the emergency crew. Supplies flying, they worked on Ted.

Over near the kitchen door, Buddy cradled Violet as, shaking, she buried her face in his shirtfront. Hillary suspected she would have crumpled to the floor had it not been for Buddy holding her together.

The crowd bunched in close. Walt had arrived with some backup deputies in uniform. Some guests gathered their things and left the parish hall, tugging at the hands of children who wanted to go see what was happening.

Hillary forced herself to take mental snapshots, feeling numb as she watched the team from the fire department, bent over Ted for long minutes. The desserts stood half eaten, the ice cream melting into milky pools.

After what seemed like hours, the paramedics shook their heads, gathered up their equipment and left the hall.

Ted lay motionless on the parish hall floor, his face a bluish gray.

* * *

Hillary stared at the coroner's van as it pulled away from the church. She wondered how she was going to cover this shocking turn of events for *The Acorn*. A few people stood around in small groups, bewildered and trying to make sense of what had happened, but the cold and the rain were swiftly dispersing them. The parking lot emptied. Hillary felt drained.

Joanna came out of the hall, her arm around Violet's waist. Violet's head hung down inside the black hood of a jacket, her face hidden. She seemed limp as a rag doll. Buddy followed close behind them. Joanna nodded in Hillary's direction, so she walked over to them. "I'm so sorry," she said. She worried they would think she was just trying to get a story but she needed to know. "What happened to him?"

Buddy frowned at Hillary. "Pretty sure it wasn't related to the food."

"What could that have to do with it?"

"Spices and nuts. They can be triggers for some people." He took his glasses off and wiped them with a handkerchief, doing little besides smearing the rainwater around. He said they were taking Violet out to Joanna's.

Hillary nodded. This was a man to be trusted. Not one of the Broomes but someone who loved one of them. A competent man. The three of them walked off.

* * *

Hillary looked for Ed and found him saying good-bye to his partner Walt, who was holding the funeral guest book wrapped in a plastic envelope.

"Thanks, pal, for getting the names." Ed patted Walt's shoulder as his partner got into an unmarked sheriff's car and drove off.

"What are the names for?" Hillary asked.

"To follow up if Ted's death turns out to be suspicious."

"That's not likely, is it?"

"No." Ed's face took on that bloodhound expression, as serious as she'd ever seen him. "But not impossible either."

"Buddy just mentioned he was concerned over the food," she said. "But I'm wondering about that deranged man who ran in with the mold signs."

"Hate it that we let him get away," Ed said. "If we'd apprehended him, we could have at least charged him with disturbing the peace."

"You did a good job with the crowd." Hillary reached for Ed's hand and, fingers locked, they went back inside the parish hall.

"What a family you've got going," Ed said, his green eyes dark with concern.

Hillary sighed. "My dad was a quiet bookworm—I'm finding out these people are so different. Now Ted is gone, before I got to know him. I can't believe it!" Hillary led the way through the deserted hall into the kitchen.

One of the aunties was putting clean dishes into the cupboards, while the other one was getting plates ready for Aunt Helena to load into the restaurant-sized dishwasher. As soon as she saw Hillary, she began babbling. "Honey, that was no accident, you ask me. Violet put enough paprika into that newfangled goulash to kill a Leipzig stallion!"

"Aunt Helena, what are you saying?" Hillary looked around the messy counter and tried to estimate how much time it would take to finish cleaning. She had to get a story up on *The Acorn* website.

"The way Teddy used to break out in hives from eating too much kolach. He always played it down, but Violet should of remembered. My goulash wasn't authentic enough for her and Joanna, no! Had to go to the Czech place over in San Francisco. Devil town, I call it."

"She wouldn't hurt her own twin," Hillary said. She had yearned for a sibling over the years. She couldn't fathom harming a brother or sister. She wondered if Aunt Helena might be getting senile in her eighties now, and on the paranoid side.

The other aunties didn't even seem to listen as Helena rambled on. "Not sure why, but mark my words, using that recipe was a bad idea." She scrubbed hard at a huge pot in the kitchen sink. "You see how red that is? I can barely get it off! Now, my goulash was mild and slick." She rinsed the copper scrubber and returned to work on the sides of the kettle, muttering under her breath.

Ed opened a couple of kitchen drawers. "Maybe we should gather some, in case it's needed to test." He pulled out a box of food storage bags and tore one off the roll. "Here, give me the scrubber, Aunt Helena, it's still got a lot packed in there."

"What will I scrub with? Can't you take some leftovers off the plates?" She turned to her sister Mary, who held up a plate.

"It's all been scraped off or eaten up, none left," Ed said. "Looks like it was popular."

"Humph. Mine was popular too!" Aunt Helena frowned and sighed. "You're the lawman." She turned over the copper scrubber to Ed, who put it in a plastic bag and sealed it.

"I'll give it over for testing later in case the autopsy shows a need for it." He rolled up his shirt sleeves, plucked a dishcloth off the counter, and began helping Aunt Helena scrub at the sides of the big pot.

Hillary's cheeks warmed. She suspected Ed would be a good fit in the family, what there was left of it now that her father, both his brothers, and suddenly Ted, too, were all gone.

Weary, she sprawled in a chair near the kitchen doors. Her father had been hit with a massive coronary. Then just six months later, his brother, Uncle Robert, keeled over with the same thing. Both of them should have taken better care of themselves, should have heeded the warning from their brother John's death five years before. All three brothers were workaholics, probably alcoholics. Hillary recalled nights waiting up for her father when he was downtown, contacting news sources, coming home to kiss her goodnight, reeking of that spicy smell she later recognized as Jack Daniels.

It couldn't have been Violet killing her own brother like Aunt Helena suggested. Those old aunties might have dementia coming on. But they could still clean up a kitchen in no time, Hillary thought, coming out of her daze, impressed as Aunt Mary marched over to lift her coat and purse off a hook near the door.

Ed approached Hillary and whispered, "Who's taking the aunties home?" He had a large wet blotch on the front of his shirt. She nodded at his stomach and smiled. "You should have put on an apron. Aunt Mary's car, how do you think they got here?"

Hillary and Ed made sure the three women left safely before they got into Ed's unmarked sheriff's car. He always drove around in it, he'd explained, even though technically they weren't supposed to. Just in case he needed to jump into his detective role. She wondered if that would happen more often around this newfound family of hers.

FIVE

Hillary

HILLARY FELT ANXIOUS about asking Ed to drive her over to the office. They didn't have any plans, but he probably didn't expect her to be working. They'd already run a lengthy obituary on Robert in *The Acorn*, but Ted's stunning collapse ratcheted up the news value of the day's event. A hot mix of elation and panic threaded her veins at the notion this story might go big, draw attention to her byline. The fear that her former boyfriend might notice her success still hounded her.

Last May, she'd moved back from the East Coast, hoping to escape Charles' threat to expose her. So far, he'd only sent benign emails, but sometimes he included a copy to the English department chair, her boss at Clearwater College. And if he found out, he might fire her. She'd cobbled together a bare-bones income as part-time reporter and part-time faculty advisor for the student newspaper.

Ed kept his face trained on the road, his profile dim against the dark sky. *Is he thinking I'm too much trouble?*

"I wouldn't need to do this if Ted hadn't . . ." Hillary felt like she was whining, begging a favor. She swallowed the wrong way and began to cough. Still Ed said nothing.

"It's just that Roger's away this weekend, some holiday party in San Francisco," she continued. "I probably need to get this up onto the *Acorn* website. BC is a pretty big company to lose two CEOs in one week."

"Hey," Ed said. He reached over to slide his hand down between her shoulder and the seatback. He began to rub her back in small circles. "No problem, Chickadee. I'm used to being out on calls all hours. No worries."

She leaned forward, warming to his touch. *Chickadee?* Where did that come from? Okay, he wasn't irked. She should have driven her own car to Uncle Robert's funeral, but who could have known his son would also be dead by the end of the day? It could be tricky to cover this story, being part of the family herself. And sad to lose Ted before she got a chance to know him.

"Not sure . . ." she said, arching her back as he kneaded her shoulder. She leaned forward to guide his hand further toward the middle of her back with each stroke. ". . . how to write up this story." She could get used to his massages. "What did Ted die from, do you think?"

He pulled his hand away and gripped the steering wheel in a 10-2 position. "Hate to say it, but might need a full investigation," he said.

"Full investigation?"

"Possible homicide." He looked over at her, his jaw set.

"Mmmmm," she murmured, her mind racing. She pawed through her tote for her cell phone and punched in Roger's number, dreading the thought of disturbing his time off—he took so little of it. He was away in San Francisco now, getting together with friends to plan something fun for next year's Gay Pride parade. She listened through six rings, waiting for the leave-a-message, but suddenly Roger came on. "Dopey, thought you knew not to call me here unless extremis is in full force?" His voice sounded slightly slurred but not by much.

"Sorry, Grumpy." It was a comfort they'd hung on to nicknames from their Sac State University newsroom days—used sometimes in fun and other times in irritation. "We've had a sort of extreme situation here."

His voice took on a sharper edge. "Not another murder with body parts on display?"

"No, nothing as definite as those killings, but . . ." She could hear hoots and hollers in the background, yelling for Roger to get back to the game, whatever that meant. "This time it's Ted—Theodore actually—son of Robert Broome, the builder."

"Isn't that your family—the Broomes?"

"Yeah, Robert was my father's brother. You know, we carried his obit last week. But at the reception after his funeral, the room broke out in chaos when his son Ted keeled over, clutching his throat and writhing as if in a seizure. EMTs couldn't save him. Problem is, we don't know the cause."

"So," Roger shot back, "you're not sure if you can cover this objectively?"

"Well, I think I can but wanted to run it by you, Grumps."

"Write it as news under my name and then a sidebar from your view as a family member," he snapped. "Call back and read 'em both to me before you upload." His voice was muffled as he called out to his friends that he was coming, a line greeted by loud guffaws. The phone went dead.

Hillary sighed and turned to Ed. "I might have to be working for an hour or so," she said, wondering what he would do in the meantime. *Jeez. I should have brought my own car.*

Ed turned in the direction of the *Acorn* office. "After we get you settled, I'll run over to our North County substation. Get Aunt Helena's scrubber routed to the lab, check in with the coroner. Call me when you're done. I'll come running." He laughed a throaty chuckle. Reminded Hillary of her father's belly laugh when he was tickled over something she'd done that made him proud.

* * *

Once they got inside the little newspaper office, Ed made sure the window blinds were closed and those covering the glass doorfront, too. He checked the storage room and the bathroom before he stood facing her. He cupped her face in his lean hands, warm to the touch. Hillary wished she didn't have this work to do.

"Don't you open the door to anyone, hear?" Ed's brows furrowed. He learned close and rubbed noses with her, then brushed his cheek lightly against hers. She closed her eyes, loving the feel of his stubbly skin.

"I'll be back soon as you call." He tapped his fingertip twice against her lips and left, wiggling the old-fashioned doorknob from the outside to check the lock.

Hillary sat at her computer. She twisted up her hair and fastened it in back with a fat black pencil from the cupful on her desk. Normally a brief story about the funeral would have run on an inside page of Roger's weekly, but the death of Theodore Broome would push it to the front. Editorial judgment—where to place pieces in the paper—was a challenge, one she shared with her journalism students over at Clearwater College.

She finished the straight news story and called to clear it with Roger. Up it went front and center on the *Acorn* website. Another scoop. The news services might pick it up since Broome Construction was such a big player in the hot housing industry, getting hotter by the month.

She took a minute to check her email. *Shit*. What she dreaded—another message from Charles. Nothing in the subject line. She peered at it. There was no cc copy to the college department chair. This time.

But she couldn't stop to read Charles' poison. Not right now, anyway. Last month, he'd attached a news clip about the firing of a Colombia professor who'd been caught plagiarizing. His subtle threat was to copy in her department chair. Luckily, that time, her chair must have assumed it was part of the nationwide campaign against plagiarism. Charles knew any hint of an ethical breach by Hillary could squash her chances to get on permanent full-time faculty with the college.

Her stomach tightened. What if she just deleted this new email from him? She stood up and poured herself a glass of tap water from the storage room sink. *I'm going to have to face it. Just not now.*

She had to write that sidebar from her view as Robert Broome's niece and Ted's cousin. What an unruly set of relatives these were. Maybe she should start writing a memoir of her father's family—an amazing success story starting with Grandad Patrick coming to America back before World War II.

Horrible that she could never do that for her mother's family—where in the world was her mother anyway? Still in the Pacific on some island? A lump of grief formed in her throat but she had no time to cry. She yanked her mind off those painful questions.

She wrote the sidebar including a sort of brief outline of the family tree, got Roger's editorial blessing, and uploaded it to the *Acorn* website. The more she thought about it, the better the idea of writing a memoir about this crazy family sounded.

She let her mind drift back to her childhood memory of the Broomes. It was the first Christmas after Mother left. Daddy had put up a tree and a bulging stocking hung on the mantel in the morning, but all Hillary could do was sit and stare at the ornament with the photo of her mother inside a clear glass ball. Suddenly, Daddy announced they were going to Lodi for Christmas dinner at Grandad Patrick's house. He'd hustled her into the car and sang along with Christmas music for the hour-long drive. But Hillary hadn't cracked a smile.

The buzz of her cousins' loud voices, teasing and laughter had cheered her up, and she began yearning to be accepted into the lively and mysterious brood. But after that, Daddy kept them to themselves, just the two of them, up in Sacramento.

Why had he kept them apart?

She sat staring at her computer screen without seeing anything.

Suddenly, the screen saver threw up a photo of a tree frog on a vivid green leaf, and she realized how late it was. Charles' email slipped easily out of her mind. She phoned Ed. "Offer for a pickup still on, Detective?" He chuckled and said he'd be right over.

* * *

After Ed helped her lock up the office, he took 99 south toward her place in Morada, making an unsuccessful attempt to stifle a couple yawns.

"Don't do that!" Hillary stretched her arms over her

head. They were not far from her cottage, headed down the dark frontage road off the highway. She felt like tickling him to keep them awake and reached over to waggle her fingers against his shirtfront.

"Hey, lady, disorderly conduct on an officer's against the law." He turned into the gravel driveway, shut off the engine, and took her hands. Pulling them to his lips, he kissed every knuckle, and lingered at her ring finger. The diamond he'd placed there on Thanksgiving sparkled even on this moonless night.

Ed spread open her hands to kiss the tip of each finger. She leaned back against the headrest, eyes closed, a little moan escaping her throat. How far should she let this go? *Holy Mary, Mother of God. Pray for us sinners.* Her judgment had been so bad in the past. Sure they were engaged but she'd been engaged to that weird Tom, too, and look how that had turned out. She turned to Ed. "I'm sure you're famished, detective. Would you like to come in for a bite?"

Laughing, they got out of the car.

* * *

After setting a cast iron frying pan on flames turned up high, she opened her cupboard and took out a can of corned beef hash. She waved it in his direction. "Look okay?" At his nod, she used a can opener on one end and flipped it to do the other end. "Come up with anything on Ted's death?" She pushed the compact cylinder of diced meat and potatoes out onto a cutting board.

"It looks like a complicated situation. The autopsy will be Monday morning, but I'm sure samples will have to be sent to toxicology. So we won't know the cause of death right away." He watched as she sliced the hash into thick rounds and set them to sizzle in the skillet. "Smells good!"

"You up for a couple fried eggs on top?" She raised her eyebrows.

"I'm up for anything from you," he teased.

"Anything?" She turned the hash circles over to brown the other side and cracked eggs, one at a time into the big skillet, biting her lip in concentration. She could feel his eyes watching her every move. "Sunny-side up?"

"Yup. Just the way I feel when I'm with you, Chickadee." He stood.

She loved his intensity. But it might be more than intense once the family legal battles started. "We already had orders to be at the lawyers Monday for Robert Broome's will." She flipped the eggs over. "Horrible as it is to say, now that Ted's gone, there might be a fight over who's going to run the business."

He walked up behind her, sliding his hands around her waist. "Looks like you're pretty good at running things."

"Come on, watch out around the fire." She snuggled her backside up against him. "Speaking of fire . . ." She turned to look at him. *Holy Mary, those green eyes.* "Fire," she repeated, "should we wait until we're married and be good Catholics?"

He nuzzled her neck. "We could always be bad ones

and go to confession."

She shook free from his embrace and laughed. Neither of them was really a good or a bad Catholic. "Go on now, Mr. Detective, sit back down." She carried his plate to the table, two circles of crispy browned hash topped by two sunny-side up eggs. "Catsup?" She set the plate on the table then put her arms around him from behind his chair.

He rubbed the back of his head against her breasts and groaned. "Let's run off to Reno," he said. "Tomorrow's Sunday, both our days off. How about it?"

She was shocked. "So soon?" she whispered. She felt dizzy. Her breath left her.

He jumped up from the table and got down on one knee. "Please, Hilly, be my wife. Now."

She pulled him to his feet in a hug. "But we haven't even known each other two months," she said. She pressed her cheek against his, inhaling the woodsy scent of his skin. "Don't we need a longer engagement?"

"This is special," he murmured. "We're old enough to know what we want."

She knew she wanted him. "All right," she laughed. "But let's at least wait until next week. I've got Roger and the students to think of."

"You win," he said. He held her tight and breathed deep against her throat.

For a while, she forgot about her hunger for the hash and eggs, cooling on the table.

SIX

Hillary

HILLARY ARRIVED FIRST at the Stockton branch office of Crocker, O'Reilly & Black, early as usual when a story was in the air. She walked into the law office at nine thirty and followed the receptionist back to a large conference room.

"May I record the proceedings?" Hillary asked the young woman, who said she'd have to check with the attorneys.

Hillary took a quick count of the number of chairs at the long, dark table. A dozen, with a few more set around the perimeter of the room. A cup and a glass sat at each place along with carafes of water and coffee, complete with cream and sugar. The basket of croissants looked inviting, but Hillary didn't want to be distracted.

She sat facing the door, to have a good view as family members entered. The receptionist returned and told her Mr. Pappas said it was all right by the terms of the will to record the reading, but he would need to let everyone know.

Hillary's heart pounded as she set up her new digital recorder. Roger had finally relented and allowed the *Acorn* to pay for this latest in electronic gadgets to cover news events. She got out a long narrow reporter's notepad, too, plus one of her favorite fat black pencils.

Within five minutes, Violet arrived along with Buddy, closely followed by Joanna and Milan. All four faces were as serious as they'd been on Saturday, not a smile among them.

Soon Aunt Helena and her five other daughters— Joanna's younger sisters—bustled in, circulating to give hugs all around. Hillary had a chance to put names to the faces of her young cousins as they told a funny story to go along with each sister's name. Their love for each other was clear, the way they nodded as they finished each other's sentences.

The isolation of being an only child stabbed Hillary in the heart. What would her life have been like if she'd had a sister? The girls poured themselves coffee and water, munched on muffins and croissants and lightened up the atmosphere. Hillary had never been to a will reading before, but these girls made it seem more like a party.

The mood fell dark, though, when Maggie walked

in, chin high, eyes blazing. She strode to the head of the table. The peacock feather in her hat added inches to her petite frame and authority to her posture, as if she were taking the place of her newly deceased husband. Her son Theodore would have been at the head of the table, but his sudden death Saturday left the chain of command uncertain. As she looked around at the family members, Maggie nodded in general recognition but smiled at no one. Hillary was almost afraid of this woman she barely knew, her aunt by marriage.

With an air of ownership, two men came in carrying legal-sized manila folders and stood directly across from Hillary. The receptionist followed, pulling a cart stacked with folders. She gave one of the thick packets to each of the relatives.

One of the lawyers, a chunky man in his sixties, raised his hands, index fingers pointed up, as if he were conducting a choir rehearsal and expected everyone to follow his directions. He pinched his right thumb to index fingertip and formed a teardrop in the air, while with his left index finger, he tapped on his copy of the document.

"Welcome, Broome Family," he began. "For those who don't know me, I'm Albert Pappas. Call me Al. And this," he gestured to the man at his side, a bit younger and slimmer than himself but dressed in a nearly identical dark suit, "this is Mike Finney. We are honored to be part of the team entrusted to take care of legal matters for the family ever since Patrick Broome incorporated back during the Second World War with the help of Sean

O'Reilly, one of the founding partners of Crocker, O'Reilly & Black."

Maggie flashed a bright smile at the attorney. She reached out and poured herself a cup of coffee, adding cream and stirring it with a flourish.

"Please read along in your copy of Robert's Will," Al said. "I'm starting on page four." He waited while the others found it.

"As you can see, the will stipulates that the reading can be recorded." He nodded in Hillary's direction. "Miss Broome has requested and therefore been granted permission to record."

Hillary held her breath, hoping no one would object.

Maggie asked in a shrill tone, "What can a recording be used for?"

"There is no stipulation on that issue," the other lawyer said. Hillary noted the two of them worked together smoothly, as if one person.

"I don't like that," Maggie shot back.

"I'm sorry, but it's there in black and white." Al Pappas raised the document and pointed to a section on page four.

Maggie frowned. "We will have to watch our tongues, then." She shook her head and grimaced, wrinkling her nose, the peacock feather bobbling for a few seconds. She refilled her coffee.

"So, carrying on . . ." Al looked around the room but wasn't reading from the text of the legal document. "The originator of this irrevocable trust, Patrick Broome, insisted that it be read aloud each time there was a change in the status of the trustees," Al said. "I was expecting to gather you all together this week after the death of Robert, in order to install Theodore in his rightful place, so I am deeply shocked and grieved over his unexpected demise." Al turned to the console behind him and picked up a box of tissues, which he placed in the middle of the table.

The family looked deadly serious, dry-eyed every one.

"I've never seen a man work so hard to control the destiny of his company from beyond the grave as did Patrick Broome." Al cleared his throat. "This trust was drawn up after World War II by Sean O'Reilly, God rest his soul, and I only had cause to turn to it when Patrick himself passed. After that, Robert ran the company with the aid of his brother John, while it should be noted their brother Gerald was specifically not included." Hillary again felt that odd mixture of shame and pride in her father, such a maverick.

"As you who are gathered here today may or may not know," Al continued, "Mr. Broome was a leader in promoting traditional family values." Al cleared his throat again and took a sip of water. "I generally don't make editorial comments, but the length he went to in binding his heirs to having a male descendant run his enterprise was exemplary. In fact, it has been cited in several legal texts as one pole of a continuum of range of control beyond the grave."

Hillary watched Maggie puff up her scrawny chest

and smile.

"So getting to the nut of the matter," Al said, "Patrick had expected that Theodore would produce male heirs for the company, but of course that will not happen now." He paused to look down the table at Maggie.

At that, she teared up and reached out for the box of tissues. "I tried . . ." She dabbed at her cheeks and bowed her head.

"In any case," Al went on, "only in the circumstance in which we find ourselves today is control of the company to pass into the hands of a female, who must be of sound mind, same as in the case of a male." The lawyer sniffed and turned in Violet's direction.

She grabbed Buddy's hand and held it clenched in hers. "Violet Broome," Al now read verbatim from the will, "as next in line in the third generation of Patrick Broome's family, inherits controlling interest in Broome Construction Corporation." He nodded quickly as if his head was a gavel pounding on the air below his chin. "Otherwise known as BCC." He pronounced each letter as a separate word, looking right at Violet. "You are entrusted to this position until a male heir appears with a legitimate claim to inheritance, either by blood or by adoption. The line of inheritance for the fourth generation starts out in this order: your son, Joanna's son, Hillary's son."

Maggie let out a loud "Ah!" and stood. "What about me?"

"You?" The lawyer's head swiveled to her end of the table. "You?"

"You said by adoption is legitimate."

"Yes. So?"

The room was quiet as a cave. Hillary held her breath.

"I'm in the process of getting twin teenaged boys as foster children, with the intention of adoption." She glared steadily at Violet.

Hillary sensed the room grow dark, as if someone had turned off the lights.

Silence held for a long minute.

Violet jumped up and pointed at her mother. "You never thought for one second about foster children, you greedy witch!"

Maggie grinned broadly, her eyes crinkling as if in real joy. "How would you know? You don't even keep in touch with your own mother who raised you."

"Your heart's too weak for that and you know it!" Violets' face turned red.

Buddy stood up and took hold of Violet's elbow. "Can we take a break?" he asked the lawyer, who nodded.

"We don't need a break," Violet whispered. "Just get on with this mess."

Mike Finney waited for Violet to sit down before he took a turn reading from the legal document, rubbing his fingertips over the stack of pages as if blessing them. Hillary was glad the recorder was going since her shock over the outbursts from mother and daughter had interrupted the flow of her notes.

Mike pointed out the percentage of shares of BCC that each family member would now own. Ten percent would go to Maggie herself as the widow of one of Patrick's sons and similarly ten percent to Aunt Helena as another son's widow. Hillary was stunned to hear that her mother got one percent as the wife of Gerald, son number three. *Is my mother really getting that money? Who sends out the dividends? Someone must have her address.*

The lawyer's voice droned on. Ever since Gerald Broome, Hillary's father, had spurned Patrick's effort to get him into the company, he had been cut off with one dollar. All the others, including spouses Buddy and Milan, got one percent of the company. A special ten percent went to the family member most engaged in the developmental basketball team in Stockton that Patrick had started in his old age. Aunt Helena's oldest daughter, Ruth, had already been given this role in the family.

Hillary noted Milan keeping track of all these numbers, in line with his role as financial officer in BCC. All this accounting left sixty percent for the controlling interest. This went to Violet, along with the power of being the managing partner.

"Well, that's the long and short of it," Al said. "Violet is now running the company. If and when male heirs come along, we will revisit these issues. The key point is the order they come up in, so yes, Margaret," he nodded in Maggie's direction, "I apologize for omitting you earlier. Any further issue from your line would be first since you were a mother of the third generation. However, if you adopt, we would have to decide on the legalities since Robert is no longer here to be the adoptive father."

Maggie grinned across the table at her daughter Violet. "What if I can show papers that he signed with the intention to do such an adoption?"

Al pushed the knot of his tie up tighter against his throat. "That would be another matter. Do you have such papers?"

She looked him straight in the eye. "Yes, sir. Indeed I do."

Violet leaped up, pushed her heavy chair back a few inches and shrieked, "Liar, liar, liar!" Leaning across the table, Violet pointed at Maggie. "You're no mother at all!"

Hillary felt the blood in her veins run cold. This was how she had dreamed of screaming at her own mother all these years, ever since she'd run off. Hillary felt light-headed.

Al ignored Violet's outburst and continued in his smooth baritone. "However, any heir must reach the age of eighteen before he can take control of the company, per the Trust language."

Violet's hands started shaking, her chin fell to her chest and she slumped into her chair. Buddy cupped his arm around her and shook her gently. She shuddered, tilted her face up at him with wide eyes, but said nothing.

The lawyer directed his next remark to Violet. "For now, young woman, do you possess the qualities needed and feel capable of running Broome Construction Corporation?"

In a low voice, she said, "I do."

With those words, Hillary feared her cousin Violet

was getting hitched to a sort of monster. *I do. What kind of journey can those words lead to?*

SEVEN

Violet

WITHOUT A WORD to the rest of the family, Buddy and I left the lawyer's office and headed straight for the parking lot. After the morning's ordeal, my cramps were killing me even though the curse was nearly over. I bent forward pressing the seatbelt against my belly, and asked Buddy to drive by the house to get my capsules. He brought the prescription out to the car along with a glass of water, the darling, and gave me his usual advice to make sure I didn't overdose. "Just take one," he said. I nodded, grateful for the powerful medicine.

He pointed his Mercedes north toward Brookside Country Club. I slipped in a CD. The soothing strains of Vivaldi's "Guitar Concerto in D" filled the car. I leaned against the headrest, and tried to keep my mind geared to the music's deliberate pace. We rode in silence, the car's engine soundless, Buddy leaving me to my roiling thoughts. *How could my mother have so much energy to spend on killing my dreams?*

It was a relief to finally pull into the club's parking lot and do such a normal thing as get out and walk to the clubhouse. Once seated in the club's four-star restaurant, I gazed out the windows at the 18th hole. The golfers were not letting a few drops of rain stop them. *That's how I have to be. Unstoppable.*

Buddy and I hadn't yet talked about my new role running Broome Construction. I turned to him. "It's what I wanted my whole life, but now it feels so . . ."

"You can do this. I have faith." Buddy nodded at a young waiter standing discreetly nearby. He came near without any of that annoying introducing himself by name. Suddenly, though not sure why, I cared about him, how old he was and what kind of family he came from.

"Who are you?" I asked, smiling up at him.

"Matt's the name, ma'am."

"Are you planning a career beyond this?" I gestured at the fancy dining room.

"Yes, ma'am. I'm in the Administration of Justice program at Clearwater College." He swallowed with a gulp and nodded toward our menus. "Are you ready or want a little more time?"

"How old are you?" I asked, knowing I was out of

line. I couldn't help myself.

"Eighteen, ma'am, just last month." He stood erect, pencil poised over his order pad.

"Um, hum." I looked at Buddy and nodded. "Eighteen, a significant age if there ever was one." The number of years a male must reach in order to fit into Grandad's scheme of things and run the business. I had to make sure no one fitting this description came near the family.

"We'll have the grilled salmon," Buddy said, ordering our favorite lunch item. He set his menu down on the table. "And coffee, too." The young man walked away.

"Joanna's restaurant will be in competition with this club," I said. "Imagine her saying I should go into business with her. She thought Teddy would keep me out of BC and here it turns out I'm the boss." I stared at Buddy, feeling thrilled and terrified at the same time.

"It's possible . . ." Buddy stabbed his fork into the lemon in his water to release some juice, then took a long swallow. "It could be that Joanna's goulash might have affected Ted," he said. "All that paprika plus those nuts and poppy seeds. Hard to tell, but—"

"Jesus, Buddy." My mouth went dry.

"Or could be a simple choking incident in the face of the uproar caused by that mold man."

"When will we know?" *It couldn't have been the goulash.*

"The autopsy preliminary report should be out by tomorrow afternoon. But I'm suspecting toxicology will be needed and that takes time." He forked the slice of lemon out of his glass and rested it on the side of his bread and butter plate, a white square, hand-painted with the club's logo, a pair of crossed golf clubs in the upper right corner. We had joined a few years back even though I didn't play golf. It was a way for Buddy to enjoy the money flowing in from his new investments. He'd even started to sound like a sales rep for bundled mortgages among his doctor friends.

Now I had control of Broome Construction. Have. The old warning about being careful what you wish for came to mind. I'd never had much luck getting what I wanted, until I met Buddy at that Mortenson Mortgage investment seminar a few years ago. Maybe my mental powers were stronger now that I was getting older.

But then there was my damn mother threatening to adopt boys to keep me from controlling BC. She was too old to adopt, wasn't she?

Buddy and I had to have some kids, boy kids, or running the business in the future would slide over to . . . who? Which of us cousins would have a boy baby first? Would it be Joanna? Hillary? It had to be me.

Fear tore at my belly. I couldn't eat a bite.

* * *

Buddy took me home before he went over to Lodi Medical for his afternoon appointments. I figured tomorrow was soon enough for me to show up at BC, so I Googled around for how to conceive a boy. Looked like there were several ways, some pretty messy. It was time to get serious about getting pregnant. I would turn thirty-six in January, but still, it should not be that hard. It was too soon for me to start thinking of adopting. I phoned for an appointment with a fertility clinic up in Sacramento and was happy they could squeeze me in at the end of the day.

* * *

I walked into the clinic, a cheery place with artful black-and-white photos of babies on the waiting room walls. Several women with basketball-sized bellies sat sprawled at the front edge of their chairs, a couple others read magazines, and a few chatted quietly. Two of them had some gray in their hair, which so far hadn't sprouted out for me. Good. Looked like these docs would take even those of us whose bio clocks were moving toward midnight.

Glossy literature in wall racks spelled out various ways to conceive, but I didn't see anything on how to choose the sex of a baby. If I was going to keep the company in my hands, I had to have a boy child and have one fast. It wouldn't be past Maggie's skullduggery to actually adopt, to get control away from me. The bitch.

I wouldn't be surprised if she really tried to adopt twin boys, an extra one for insurance, maybe around the age of seventeen, so they could be ready to take over soon. I had to stop that farce. Dad would not have gone so far as to sign adoption papers before he died. He didn't know he was going to die! I felt as nervous as a cat in a vet's office.

A young assistant led me down the hall and into a Dr. Randle's office. He stood and took my cold hand in his big warm one. I just loved doctors who shake hands with their patients, like Buddy does.

"So, what can I do for you, young lady?" He gestured toward one of the chairs across from his desk.

I took a seat, feeling comfortable right way. "I need help getting pregnant. We've been trying for almost a year now." I brushed my hair off my forehead and leaned toward the doctor.

"You look too young to worry about that yet." He sat back and folded his hands in his lap.

"Well, to tell you the truth," I blurted, "I need to get pregnant with a boy. Can you help people with that?"

He raised his eyebrows. "Tell me why."

"It's a family inheritance thing." I wondered what he would think of this. Was this legal or ethical from his point of view?

"Ummm. Tell me more."

"It's Broome Construction. My father died last week, and then without warning, also my brother!" I grabbed a Kleenex off his desk to dab my eyes, so he wouldn't think I was unfeeling.

"In my grandfather's trust, only males can inherit controlling interest in the company, but we don't have any men left in the family. So—" I gulped, wondering how strange this sounded—"I've been given control for now, but I need to have a boy so there will be a male heir to continue on the family name and business." I blinked a few times and held the Kleenex pressed up under my nose.

"I see. So you are a busy career woman, you're telling me?"

I nodded. He stood and walked to a bookshelf. Pulling out a slim volume, he brought it over and sat in the empty chair next to me, glancing at my left hand. "I assume we have a husband in this picture, yes?"

I nodded. "Yes. You might know him? Buddy Briggs. An allergist down in Lodi."

"No, but we will of course need his help." He smiled, and opened the thin book, containing large graphics showing the conception process. The last few pages were details of various theories on how to choose the sex of a child. "Because you're so young, we can try this method first," he said. He traced the images on the page, cartoon figures of sperm swimming in a race to reach their goal, a fat egg waiting in the fallopian tube like a queen in a throne room.

"The Y sperm," Dr. Randle went on, "those are the guys, and they swim faster than the gals, the X's. You want to have the Y's there at the right time, early on, because they die faster and are overtaken by the slower gals. If you time intercourse about twelve hours before ovulation, you've got the best chance that an aggressive guy swimmer will be the winner." He nodded as if he had invented the competition and was about to take a bow.

I was amazed. "Time it?"

"There are several ways to do it, but considering you don't want to be kept busy during the day, urinating on a stick …" He looked at me. "Do you?"

"God, no!" How weird does that sound?

He left the room and returned with a small white box wrapped in cellophane. "Just take this special thermometer home—it's called a basal body temperature thermometer—and start keeping track of your ovulation cycle. The directions are inside. You just need to take your temperature while still in bed each morning. You chart it on a form, and when you see a sudden drop in the number, that means you will ovulate within twelve hours. Grab your hubby then, and go to it." He laughed. "It can be fun, much more so than the in vitro fertilization process. Good luck!" He stood up.

"We'll have an examination first, though, make sure all your parts are in working order." He beamed.

What a slaphappy doctor, delighted with the drama of conception.

After my exam, he seemed very positive that I would be able to conceive with no trouble when using this kit.

"The key thing," he said, "is that you'll have to try to abstain from intercourse, and your husband will need to be sure not to let the little guys rush out in any other way, either." He paused to grin. "So he gets a nice big storehouse of them, say three or four days before you need them to come charging in." He nodded toward the white little box. "The details are in there. Just follow them carefully, and I'll put my money on seeing you back here in a couple months, ready to start the journey to motherhood!"

What a jolly man. If it were up to him, all people

would have a happy ending to their stories.

* * *

My heart singing, I drove home. Mother wouldn't be able to ace me out of the company, now or ever. I had just as much blood birthright as Teddy. More, really, since I was born six minutes before him. If only she'd stuck up for me like a real mother.

I opened the baby-making kit and set out the pieces on top of our dresser, a black finished credenza with a mirror above. I couldn't help but notice my reflection. My mouth was set into a flat, determined line, eyebrows furrowed into a deep V. I almost scared myself with my concentration. No baby should have to gaze upon such a stern face. I took a deep breath, held it for a count of five, and exhaled, trying to relax.

The supplies were wrapped in clear cellophane packages that crinkled as I opened the first one, a thermometer. Instead of showing the usual ten lines between the numbers 96 and 104, it had about thirty lines between 98 and 99.

Next, I opened a pad of graph paper and a brochure. The directions made it sound easy just like the doctor had said. You were supposed to not get up in the morning until after you took your temperature, then record it on the graph paper. As soon as the number dropped down near 98, you were supposed to grab your man and have sex, deep penetration preferred. That was the way to try to have a boy because those male sperms were fast swimmers and you wanted them there as soon as your temp rose again, showing that your egg was coming down the fallopian tube. If you waited more than twelve hours, then the speedy Y chromosome guys would have already died and let one of the slower but longer-lived females swim on up to pierce the egg.

Sounded simple enough. I'd never even tried to figure out my ovulation time. No wonder I wasn't pregnant yet.

* * *

After dinner, we sat in front of the fireplace while I told Buddy what I'd learned that afternoon at the Sacramento clinic.

He laughed. "Those fertility docs! They never taught us anything like that in allergy residency." He rotated his head against a sofa pillow, making popping sounds as his neck cracked. I smiled and rubbed my fingertips just below his slightly receding hairline to give a little scalp massage the way he liked it.

"The miracles of scientific research," I said. "Now we can have a boy and secure the ownership line for ourselves." He nodded, and I went on to explain that deeper penetration and my having an orgasm both favored conceiving a boy. He turned to me with a look in his eyes, suddenly a sparkling turquoise. Or maybe it was just my new way of seeing him for this project.

His voice came across in a low register, husky. "Didn't know you were so hot to trot, babe."

I laughed. "Now we can be first in line to control BC for years." I jumped up in excitement and waved my hands like a cheerleader.

"Sure you want to compete like this?" Buddy reached up for my hands and pressed them to his lips.

"You know Maggie is full of bull when she says she started adoption steps. Wouldn't put anything past her, but she never did any such thing." It was hard staying mad when my belly began to flutter from Buddy's kisses.

"How do you know?" he murmured.

"She's a selfish bitch if ever there was one. Just loves all the money and position. I'm sure she was counting on Teddy to marry his Bridget and for her to crank out a slew of baby boys."

Buddy sat back against the sofa, pulling me down against him. "Want to practice so we're ready when the thermometer gives the signal?"

"Well, my period just ended, so I won't be ovulating right now," I said. I jumped up and pulled my silk blouse over my head and tossed it toward him. "But practice never hurts!"

I ran down the hall toward our room, stripping off my bra, and crawled between the sheets. "Let's see what we can come up with, Buddy of mine," I called out.

He chased close behind and flung the covers back to expose my nakedness. I spread my arms open wide, eager to play.

Tonight, it's time for fun. Tomorrow, I become boss lady. A little happiness won't jinx this new good luck of mine.

EIGHT

Ed

MONDAY ED GOT THE CALL he'd expected from Sheriff Coats. If something suspicious turned up on the autopsy, the sheriff wanted Ed and Walt on the case, pronto. Trevor Coats attended quickly to anything connected to top donors like Broome Construction, especially since his close reelection last month.

A few hours later, the preliminary autopsy report was released. Ed was troubled to see no conclusive cause of death for Theodore Broome. The cover letter noted it could take a few weeks before toxicology reports came back.

No news was not good news.

Ed was loath to get rolling on this case involving Hillary's family. If it was a case. He was trying to wind down his workload, get away from Stockton, and drive to Reno in between storms. Plus, there were the matters of getting to Silva's Jewelry to pick out a wedding band and asking Walt to be his best man.

Ed scratched his chin. The stubble was already pushing through. Maybe he'd get one of those razors that let a five o'clock shadow show. Hillary liked that rubbed up gently against her cheeks. With the dimples.

Three sharp knocks on his desktop ended his daydream. Deputy Laurel Mendoza stood holding out a manila file folder labeled "BROOME, THEODORE."

"Got the funeral guest book names all typed up," she said, "with most of the addresses and phone numbers, head table first, then next, and so on to the back of the room. Your partner did a good job—muy bien." The young woman grinned at Walt, who scowled in return, his usual prickly self with female law officers. "Found your disturbing-the-peace guy, too," she said. "Check out page three of the guest book—what a signature."

Ed thanked his dark-haired protégé, stood with the folder tucked under his arm, and walked over to sit in a chair next to Walt's metal desk. "Witnesses. If we have a case. Damn sheriff kowtowing to his big donors." Ed pulled out the typed sheets and placed them in front of Walt. "Who should we contact first?"

"Who haven't we talked to yet?" Walt reached over for a glazed apple fritter sitting on a napkin at the far side of his desk.

Ed put his fist to his chin and cracked his neck to both sides. Walt needed to cut out junk food. Last month a suspect in the PriceCuts killings got away because neither of them was in top shape. Ed was proud of himself—he'd quit the little cigars. And he was thinking about getting a routine going at the gym.

He took the typed sheets and studied them, then pulled out the original funeral guest book from its plastic envelope. There it was on page three in block letters: MAD MOLD MAN.

Jesus.

No corresponding phone number on the typed list, of course. That guy with the sign and bullhorn got clean away.

Damn. It was his job to catch people like that. The ones who hit and run. The old shame of his daughter's killer getting away flooded through Ed's chest and arms. Five years and that driver was still on the loose. *Jesus H. Christ.*

He shook his head, cracked his neck again, and yanked himself back to the present. Theodore Broome's death might not even be a crime, for God's sake. He only had to work it because of the effing big deal Broome Corporation. He felt conflicted over being engaged to one of them. *But Hillary is so different from the others.* He scanned the typed list.

"Okay. Found Hillary." He crossed out her name. "She's clean."

He glanced at Walt, still busy with his fried pastry, a chomp at a time with a faraway look in his eyes. Ed checked off a few more people he knew couldn't be suspects.

If there was a case.

"Mortenson, Jake Mortenson," Ed read out. "Name sounds familiar. Haven't talked to him." Ed reached for Walt's desk phone and punched in the number for Mortenson.

A sugary voice sang out: "Mortenson Mortgage. We move you up."

"Detective Ed Kiffin here, San Joaquin County Sheriff's Department. Need to talk to Jake Mortenson."

She informed him that Mr. Mortenson was in a meeting but could return the call. Ed gave his number and hung up.

"What did this Mortenson guy look like?" Ed waited, tapping his pen on the desk while Walt finished off his last bite.

"Big man, about my size." Walt wiped his mouth with a napkin and burped quietly.

"He was sitting near Ted's table. Let me see that list." Walt took it from Ed, studied it, and pointed to another name. "I had them all take the seats they were in before Ted collapsed, so I could list 'em in order. This Mortenson was across from Ted at the next table. On the other side of Mortenson was this guy." Walt pointed to the name Francisco Blanco. "Him. Give him a call. Different number."

At that number, Ed got a Bank of Norcal recording but had no patience to wait and leave a message. He would get to the guy later. "This Blanco may be part of a financial group tied in to BC along with Mortenson." Ed frowned and slapped at the names with the back of his open hand. "But Ted's sister Violet benefited the most. She's running the company now."

Walt brushed specks of glaze off his white shirtfront, then gave Ed his full attention. "I saw her in the parish hall, nearly collapsed against the wall with her husband holding her up. She's a lightweight, be out of her depth trying to control a big company like BC, if you ask me."

"Yeah. Feels weird. She's Hillary's cousin." Ed found Violet's name and called the number, which turned out to be for Broome Construction. He set up an appointment for the next day.

Enough time spent on this case.

If it was a case.

Ed tossed the file on his nearby desk. "I want to get over to Silva's, get a band to go with the engagement ring I gave Hillary last month." He narrowed his eyes at Walt. "You ought to find a nice girl, someone who can cook decent food for you." Walt ignored him.

They walked out through the rain and got into Ed's unmarked. He headed toward downtown, windshield wipers clacking.

* * *

"Marcus Silva at your service." The short and cheerful owner greeted them effusively. "What can I do for you, my friends? Christmas treasures for your sweethearts?" Walt frowned and walked off toward the men's watches.

"I need a wedding band," Ed said. "Going to Reno soon."

"Congratulations!" He motioned Ed over to a case sparkling with diamonds. "Do you want to take a look, maybe bring her in later so she can select?"

Ed shook his head. The memory of the arduous process of his first wedding brought up a sour taste. He'd been instructed that a woman needed two rings, one engagement and one wedding. Thankfully, his grandmother had not yet designated who would get which pieces of her jewelry, and he hadn't wasted the antique diamond on wife number one.

That wife had become mother to his darling daughters though, now both missing from his life. One killed in a hit-and-run, the other moved out to the East Coast, poisoned against him by that first wife. Ed clenched his jaw.

He tried to visualize Hillary's hand. It was the left hand he'd put his grandmother's quarter-caret solitaire on, he was sure. What would she want for a wedding band?

An image came to mind of Hillary scribbling across the pages of her reporter's notebook. That was back in October. The investigation into the PriceCuts killings. Only a couple months and he felt he had known her forever. But her hands. She was left handed.

"I think maybe just plain gold?" *Should he wear one this time?* He wore a plain band that first time. He glanced down at his hand and recalled how it had chafed. He'd taken it off a few years later, after a Sacramento cop got hung up by his ring when jumping a cyclone fence chasing a gang member.

His wife hadn't even noticed the ring missing from his finger.

Leave it to Hillary to get me a ring if she wants.

"Right," Mr. Silva said. "You can always come back later, say on an anniversary, and get diamonds if that seems right then." Mr. Silva reached over to get a tray of simple bands and placed them on the glass countertop.

"We have a range of widths and styles. We can engrave on the inside, too, if you give us a couple hours." He cleared his throat and looked around the small shop, empty except for the three of them. "Or at least an hour."

Ed studied the rings in the tray. Silva didn't realize he'd already given Hillary a diamond, but he didn't feel like explaining. The plain rings looked like a good match, yes, but suddenly a band set with seven miniature emeralds caught his eye. Emeralds. Hillary was Irish. He was Welsh and Irish on his mother's side. His imagination fired up. Celtic countries. Maybe they could take a honeymoon over there next summer when she didn't have her journalism students.

"Her hands are smaller than mine," he said, extending his fingers for the owner's inspection. "I'm not sure of her size but it's about the same as my little finger." He'd tried his grandmother's ring on his pinkie before he'd given it to her. "Engrave inside 'EK heart HB.'"

After Ed made it clear he meant a heart-shaped symbol and not the word "heart," he dragged Walt away from the watches and they left the jewelry store. It had stopped raining.

Ed couldn't keep from grinning. He felt like a damn fool, like jumping up to click his heels together on the wet sidewalk, and an image of a leprechaun popped into his head. He looked up, hoping for a rainbow, but dark clouds filled the sky.

"I'm hungry," said Walt. "Let's stop by the deli."

Ed slid into the driver's seat and started the engine. It wasn't the time to get on Walt about his eating habits, but instead, to keep him in a good mood.

* * *

Juicy slivers of pastrami and threads of sauerkraut dangled from the caraway seed rye bread Walt had selected for his Reuben. He fingered the loose pieces outside the bread and stuffed them into the sandwich.

Ed wanted Walt to find a woman to get him onto a better way of eating. Fueled by the heat of his romance, Ed felt glowing with health. His craving for cigars had faded in his flush of eagerness to get Hillary into his arms and devour her with kisses. He couldn't get enough of her spicy perfume. Just the thought of being with her was enough to calm him down and excite him at the same time.

Ed took a bite of his bagel with lox and cream cheese and pondered what else he needed to get ready for the three-hour drive to Reno. Or maybe they should drive to Tahoe's South Shore? No, Reno was more for weddings, he thought. His first wife had dragged him through a formal Catholic wedding and look how that turned out. She divorced him four years ago, not long after he failed to find the hit-and-run killer of their daughter. Lord knows he had tried. And he damn sure hadn't given up.

He sighed and stared at Walt, who picked up his sandwich with both hands, guarding the slippery innards from tumbling out. This was a new day, thought Ed. Time for my new life. "I know this is sudden," he said, "but can you come along to Reno? Be my best man?"

Walt reached for a napkin and wiped Thousand Island dressing off his chin. Thank God he had some sense of manners. Ed hated to think of what he looked like when eating at home alone. Walt's marriage had ended a decade ago, when his diabetic wife had died in a high blood sugar coma. You'd think that would have made him more careful about his health.

"What?" Walt set down his sandwich and took a long swallow from his mug of root beer.

"Yeah, I know it happened fast, but she's the one." Ed stared at his partner.

Walt shook his head slowly. "Look what Elizabeth did, ran out on you and took little Caron with her."

"Okay, second time around, yeah, but I have a gut feeling I can trust Hillary."

Walt took the last bite of Reuben, holding it over the white paper wrapper to catch the dripping dressing. He chewed thoughtfully and swallowed. "You know what I think about marriage, pal."

"But this is Hillary, the one who saved that nice old lady from the berserk butcher over in Lodi. Hillary's a strong woman. And healthy."

"Still, she'll want to run your life after a while. Look how free we both are these days."

"Freedom's just another word for nothing left to lose." Ed couldn't believe that Janis Joplin line had popped out so easily. It was true, though.

Walt sighed, wiped his mouth, pushed his chair back and stood. He reached out and slapped Ed on the back. "I know there's chemistry between you two." He laughed. "As long as it's not some woman cop. Go for it. Sure, I'll come with you. Who's she bringing? Someone for me?" He bellowed a booming laugh. "Who would want this?" He spread his hands over his generous belly. "I need to try to get on that new show, *The Biggest Loser*! I'm hooked on it, but all I do is feel grateful I'm not as bad off as those poor bastards."

"Don't know, man," Ed said. "Got to get you to the gym after New Year's." Ed fantasized the workouts he himself was going to be getting, at night. The wedding party was starting to shape up. Ed's chest swelled with joy.

* * *

The next morning, Ed suggested he and Walt go talk to Mortenson and Blanco, the mortgage banker guys. It wouldn't hurt to make some connections that might help in financing a house later. Hillary's cottage was tiny and his apartment was just a rundown studio.

Walt copied the two addresses from the file and they took off.

Ed drove down a wide street in Stockton's financial district, or what there was of one. He pulled up in front of a restored building that housed Mortenson Mortgage and set the magnetic emergency light on top of the car to ensure against a parking ticket, make it easy on the meter maid.

The lobby was decorated with scenes out of Stockton's past, including Gold Rush images. It exuded the scent of old money in that mysterious way some aged buildings do.

A young male receptionist greeted them. After learning of their business, he phoned for Mr. Mortenson's okay, then nodded them toward a set of double doors recessed off to the right of the lobby.

A portly bald man stood just inside, beaming a wide smile, his thumbs hooked into little pockets on his charcoal pinstriped vest. Ed recognized him, a living stereotype of a mortgage banker. The guy looked the same as he did the day of Robert Broome's funeral, as if he never slept or changed clothes but stood in a corner all night every night, not to rumple his façade.

"Want to ask you a couple questions, Mr. Mortenson." Ed stood, notepad in hand. The banker smiled and led them back to his ample office.

"Have a seat, gentlemen." Mortenson gestured toward a couple of club chairs in front of his desk. "Always a pleasure to assist the law."

Walt and Ed remained standing. "It's about the day of Robert Broome's funeral," Ed said. "Theodore didn't seem pleased to see you there. Can you say why?"

"Well, frankly, the young man wasn't very enthusiastic about promoting loans for his housing business. He needed educating about creative financing, sorry to say." He smiled and blinked slowly as if his meaning was obvious.

Ed changed his focus to the food. "Did you see anyone put anything in Theodore's drinks or food at the wake?"

Mortenson blinked rapidly. "In his food? It wasn't natural causes, then?"

"We need to look into it, sir. Appreciate your cooperation." Ed shifted from his left to his right foot.

"In his food. You mean sprinkle something on it or what?" Mortenson stood up. "I better ask Mr. Wagner. He might have seen something. My mind is in the clouds sometimes, you know?" He pushed his intercom buzzer and asked the receptionist to tell Wagner to come in.

"What about you, yourself, though?" Walt asked.

"Me? Well, I was shocked to have Theodore go into that . . ." He looked back and forth from one detective to the other. "Fit. Was it a fit? Seemed like an epileptic fit, maybe?"

The double doors opened and in strode a younger version of Mortenson. "Officers. What can I do for you?" Wagner stood at Mortenson's side.

Ed repeated his questions. Wagner said he had not

seen anyone fiddling over any dinner food. "After, though, when they put out the desserts . . ." he began.

Walt cleared his throat and pulled his handkerchief from his pocket to wipe his mouth.

Wagner gazed at Walt, then continued. "BC's designer, that blonde woman sitting next to us, she walked up front and was stirring his coffee, I noticed. Just thought she was fixing it the way he liked it, same as I'd seen her do over at their building. Know what I'm saying?" He winked at Ed.

"What do you mean?" Ed stood perfectly still.

"Well, you know, she was happy to serve up coffee along with her design services." He grinned. "Not sure what else she served up."

Ed nodded and jotted onto his notepad. "Her name?"

"Donna. Donna Lister. The receptionist can get you her address."

"Anyone else do anything out of the ordinary?" Ed was now itching to get over and interview that blonde.

"Of course, that protester was right next to Theodore, waving around that sign and his bullhorn. Creep."

"Know him? Seen him before?" Ed asked.

"He looked familiar. Might have been on television or something. You know, you just can't make every single homeowner happy."

"Meaning?"

"Robert, God rest his soul, took it hard, those sour-grape buyers imagining they had mold issues or such." He stood closer to Mortenson, hand on the older man's

shoulder. Ed thought they looked like some kind of fa-
ther-and-son *American Gothic* painting.

"How can we get a list of disgruntled buyers?"

"We only service the mortgages, fold them into investment bundles. It's a good deal, if you officers want in
on it." He smiled and slapped Mortenson on the back.

"No, thanks." Ed sensed something was wrong with
this picture. "I need names."

"Afraid you'll have to go over to Broome for those.
Again, we don't hang on to the paper. We work with
high-level companies that pick up our bundled mortgages. You officers really should think about getting into
this boom market." He beamed as if he'd just invented a
money machine. "I can get you a slice of the pie for less
than the usual minimum twenty-five thousand."

"Thanks. We may be in touch again." Ed handed
out his card to the men, as did Walt. They left the old
building, took the portable light off the roof of the unmarked, and got back in.

"Something's rotten in Stockton," said Ed. "Smells
like part of a big mess, I'm afraid." He started up the car
and drove away. They had some information now. But it
was just a piece. How big was this puzzle? If it was a case,
that is.

Ed was looking forward to what they might learn
from blonde Donna.

NINE

Ed

ED GOT WALT to give Donna a heads-up call while he drove toward the address in an industrial section. She had made no secret of her identity, signing the funeral guest book with her name and adding "Broome Design Consultant."

Ed pulled into a parking space in front of a warehouse-type building. Inside the front door was a tiny entrance partly screened off from a workroom full of tables with textiles spread out on them and furniture in groupings around the perimeter. Drapes and carpet squares hung from the walls. No one was in the entrance, so Ed and Walt walked back and spotted the woman who must be Donna. She was moving swatches of fabric around on what looked like an old ping-pong table.

Ed and Walt moved toward her but were intercepted by a young man with spiky black hair and a few studs poking from above his shaved eyebrows. "Can I help you?"

"We need to talk to Donna." Ed nodded toward her.

At the sound of the deep voices, she looked up and stretched. Ed couldn't help but notice her curvy figure, clad in an orange stretch jumpsuit. She walked in their direction, adjusting the layout of a carpet square on one of the tables as she closed the twenty feet between them.

Both men showed their badges. "Is there somewhere we can go?" Ed asked. "We have a few questions, ma'am."

She looked toward the back of the large space. "We can go to the break room. I like to have somewhere to get away from all this clutter." She laughed a throaty chuckle. "I meet clients in the BC Design Center, never in here. They'd think I was too disorganized." She pointed to where she wanted them to follow. "Art is messy, don't you know?"

She led the way, stopping to lay her hand on a stack of fabrics and furniture brochures. "I've got a couple ideas started for Violet Broome. Word's out at BC she's running the show now and her father's office will never do for her. Sad about her father going so suddenly"—her voice caught for a second—"and then Teddy."

"Teddy?" Ed wondered about her use of the nickname.

"Ted." She cleared her throat. "Theodore. He had some of us call him Teddy."

Ed and Walt followed her to a back room crowded with an eclectic mix of furnishings. A daybed covered with decorator pillows in many colors was pushed up against a far wall next to a counter. Boston Red Sox and Notre Dame sports mugs stood on a table next to the large bed.

A small refrigerator stood on the counter complete with a sink and littered with a microwave, an empty glass coffeepot, and an electric teakettle. Donna pushed a lever on the kettle and turned to gesture toward an armoire. "Keep clothes in here for times I stay overnight. Even got a bath with shower, behind that curtain." She nodded toward a far corner.

The spiky-haired young man had followed them, glaring but silent.

"It's okay, Byron, you can get back to the job." She smiled and waved him out. "He's a sweet boy. Protective. The neighborhood can get rough so I like to get boy interns from the design program over at Clearwater College." She laughed and turned to pour herself a cup of hot water and pull out a teabag from a box on the counter. "Can I get you officers a cup of tea? Coffee?" She stirred Splenda into a delicate white cup and looked at them.

"No, thanks, ma'am." Ed stood with his notepad and pen out. "We noticed you were at the service and wake for Robert Broome." He waited. Sometimes in a gap of silence people would come out and offer information. She sat down and blew on her tea.

Ed looked around the small back room. Walt cleared his throat.

She took a tentative sip from her cup while she studied the two men. "Have a seat, please." She motioned them to join her at the table.

Ed and Walt remained standing.

"Did you serve Ted coffee or anything, ma'am?" Ed maintained his serious visage. Walt raised his eyebrows and presented an open look.

"Please," she said, rubbing her fingers over the table surface, as if judging its texture. "Don't call me 'ma'am.' I'm too young for that, don't you think?" She swung her long legs out from under the table and crossed them, her orange bodysuit clinging like a second skin.

Ed found it hard to concentrate. Before Hillary had come along it was easy for him to close himself off to the allure of sexy women, but his fresh new physical connection to Hillary had opened a long-shut door.

"Ma'am," he began. "Miss," he said, feeling flustered. He looked at Walt.

"Look, Ms. Lister." Walt stepped near to Donna and looked directly into her eyes. "We just need you to tell us what you saw that day," Walt continued. "We know you were sitting near Ted. Can you tell us what happened before he collapsed?"

Donna stood and opened a drawer at the counter, pulling out a red paper napkin and blotting her lips. "Well, he did eat a lot. I hadn't seen him before in his whole family setting." She sat back down, napkin clenched in her fist. "In fact, it was shocking what a glutton he was that day." She grimaced and looked at Walt, who nodded. "But no, I didn't serve him anything. Wish I were part of the family that got to, though." She sighed.

Ed scribbled notes on his pad, relieved that Walt had taken over. *Was the banker lying about her pouring Ted coffee?*

"What was your relationship to Ted?" Walt went on in a low tone.

"Well, we worked together, you know? I was the chief interior designer for Broome Homes, the models." She smiled. "We are number one nationwide, did you officers know?"

She got up and pulled open the doors to a wall cabinet. "I don't keep these out where I can see them. Don't want to get fat and lazy." She pointed to several magazine cover pages that featured her glowing face. There were also certificates tacked to the corkboard lining inside the cabinet doors.

She returned to the table. Gazing at the open cabinet, her face took on a deep red flush. "We worked well together. Better than he did with that fiancée of his." Her pale blue eyes watered up.

Ed felt all business once more. There was something to this. "Did you know his fiancée?" he said, taking over the questioning. "Did she work with the company, as well?"

Donna sighed. "I never met her, but Ted carried photos of her in his wallet. Was always pulling them out wherever we went and showing people. Made me feel invisible, yet there I was, the faithful workhorse at his side."

Ed nodded. *She looks more like a racehorse than a workhorse.*

"This went on for months, years! She's the daughter of an East Coast developer with ties to world bankers. All kinds of men were after her for the connections to her father. But she gave the nod of her sleek black Irish head to Teddy." Donna had turned a bright crimson and was waving at her cheeks with the red napkin as if it were a fan. She dropped her head into her hands and sobbed.

Ed and Walt stood silent as seconds passed. After a minute, she raised her head and dabbed at her eyes with the napkin. "Teddy is. . . ." She stopped talking and stared dry-eyed at Ed.

"He *was* super sexy. Voted up and coming young man for *California* magazine a couple years ago." She picked up her tea cup, walked over to the antique armoire and opened it wide. Inside the door were taped images of Ted Broome. She stood looking at the outstretched fingers of her left hand, then moving them to trace the outline of Ted Broome's square-jawed face on the cover of GQ magazine.

"At first, I thought he would get over her." Donna was staring at his face, rubbing it lightly with her fingertips. "Instead, last month, he suddenly gets engaged to the *lady*." Without warning, she raised her right hand and smashed the teacup against his picture, translucent china shattering into shards and falling to the floor. She held out her hand, starting to bleed. "How could he do that? Just for money! He already had plenty."

After making sure Donna's cuts were superficial, and leaving Byron to help her, Ed and Walt left.

"There's a broad to keep our eyes on," said Walt.

"Want to go talk to another female who deserves attention," Ed said. "Got to talk to Violet, now that it looks like she's got the job of running Broome Construction. See what she might have had to do with that vacancy."

TEN

Hillary

HILLARY HAD LINGERED AROUND the law office Monday to chat with Maggie. Nervous that this aunt by marriage would cut her off, Hillary was relieved when instead she seemed open to an interview. Hillary explained that her editor wanted to run a feature story on the Broome family. Maggie agreed to a meeting set for a couple days later.

Now Hillary drove through a light drizzle along Stockton's quiet West Lincoln Road. It ran parallel to Five Mile Slough, a little creek tucked away in the midst of town. Alex Spanos, owner of the San Diego Chargers, lived here, too, but Hillary couldn't spot his address on any of the half dozen metal gates appearing every so often on the creek side of the road. Maggie's address was marked, though, and Hillary parked her VW Golf across the street from the entrance.

She gulped the last of her French roast from her car mug, her stomach queasy over meeting alone with the formidable Maggie. Outside the white picket gate, she pushed the intercom buzzer.

Maggie's voice rang out from a hidden speaker at the same time the gate latch clicked open. Once inside the compound, Hillary could see Maggie's petite figure, framed in her ornate doorway. She was clad in a pair of dark, tailored slacks, a cream-colored shell, and a black cardigan with pearl buttons along the front edge. "Don't you have enough sense to come in out of the rain?" Maggie cried out with no hint of humor.

This must be the kind of comments Violet had to put up with all her life.

Hillary followed Maggie into a living room decorated in cool tones, warmed by a fire dancing inside a white brick fireplace. An oil painting dominated the wall over the mantel.

Maggie stared up at the figures in the picture. "My three guys." She clasped her hands together and sighed. "Grandad, Robert, and little Ted."

"I'm so sorry for your losses," Hillary said, feeling awkward.

"Going to have to bury poor Ted privately now. Can't go through that hubbub again." Maggie stared expressionless at Hillary. The woman must be in shock, thought Hillary.

"But, like they say, there is a silver lining to every cloud," Maggie called out, her pale blue eyes narrowing. "And I'm busy planning a lining that might turn out to be gold." She sat on a sofa and nodded toward a matching sofa, facing hers.

Hillary was amazed the woman could sound so cavalier about burying her son. *Of course, my own mother walked out of my life without a care.*

"I'm hoping to get your insights on the family tradition of enterprise and service." Hillary knew she was laying it on thick, but Maggie was a proud woman. Besides, Roger wanted a local angle on the blazing hot housing market.

"Mind if I record our conversation?" Recalling Maggie's protest over her recording the reading of the will, Hillary's heart pounded. She set her Sony out on the glass-topped coffee table.

"That's fine, but only if you can get a copy for me." Maggie picked up a brass bell from the end table and shook it with vigor. Within seconds, a middle-aged Hispanic woman appeared. "Bring us coffee, Luisa."

Without a glance at Hillary, the woman nodded and disappeared.

"We don't generally make copies available," said Hillary, frowning. "Reporters have gone to prison rather than release tapes, but I'll see what I can do." Getting Maggie a copy would be a hassle and not standard operating procedure, but Hillary wanted to keep the interview going. "I cannot run the story by you for your approval, though. You realize that, right?"

Maggie nodded. She smiled and smoothed her cardigan across her flat chest. The housekeeper came back in, rolling a serving cart, and Maggie took a few minutes to pour them both a cup of dark brew. Maggie topped hers off with a healthy dollop of cream but Hillary shook her head when it was offered. *Glad I can stick to black coffee—the only part of the diet that's working for me.*

Rain started to beat hard against the windows but the fire cast a cozy glow inside the room.

"Of course," Maggie began, "we have a history of BC on the website and for the brochures, but it's so skimpy. What I add in today I want a copy of." She sipped at her coffee, then set down her cup and smoothed her black hair, tucking behind her ears a few strands just beginning to be threaded with gray. "You may turn on your recorder."

After setting the Sony to voice-activated, Hillary picked up her notebook and pencil to help her organize key points later on. This was her family story, too. Part of it, anyway.

"Well," Maggie started out. "Robert never talked about the past, too busy keeping up with the here and now. What he really loved was the future." Hillary thought Maggie sounded awfully unemotional talking about her late husband.

"Grandad Pat, though, when he got old, started to tell his story." Hillary felt a pang of envy. She never got to know her grandfather.

"Patrick," Maggie went on, "he was born in Ireland,

in 1910. His father was a fisherman in Galway. That place was home of the Claddagh symbol, heart and hands, you know?" Maggie reached out her small hand to show Hillary a gold ring in the shape she was describing.

"Life was hard over there." Maggie paused, watching Hillary take notes. "Along came a sister for Patrick in 1912—too bad it wasn't a brother." Maggie pursed her lips and frowned before she went on. "And they were just getting by when a mammoth storm blew up and took out half the fishing fleet, including Patrick's father. There they were, him and his mother and sister, nearly starving and trying to survive." She paused.

"Getting independence from the British caused tremendous upheavals all his young life, with so many people there divided and embittered.

"Patrick said he hired himself out to local farmers for pennies a day, he did." Maggie had fallen into a kind of Irish lilt, Hillary noticed. "He did whatever was needed, he said. That's when he learned to dig stones from the rocky soil, stack them into low walls all over the countryside, build sheds for animals and crops. Building, it started up in him then, he said.

"Soon, though, his mother got sick, real sick. His sister, Fianna, tried to care for her, but by the time Patrick turned 17, their mother was dying. He got names of relations who'd come to America before, during the potato famine. He located some of his people in San Francisco, he said." Maggie took a sip of coffee and nodded to Hillary, then looked into the fireplace and continued.

"He had to get his mother buried and then he up and took his sister and moved to California. His sister did'na want to move, had a sweetheart in Galway, a boy named James, but she was too young to leave her there alone, Patrick said." Maggie's eyes sparkled. "What a man already, and so young!

"Worked for a painting contractor in San Francisco, lived in the Irish section. Took odd jobs helping build anything," Maggie gestured air quotes with her fingers, "'anything coming up from the ground' was how he put it."

Hillary scribbled fast, keeping an eye on the digital recorder. This family history was hers, too, and she was more caught up in it than she thought she'd be. Her father had been rejected as a sort of namby-pamby book lover who didn't fit in. When he died, the isolation of being an only child had settled around her like an invisible coat.

Maggie took a long swallow of coffee, draining her cup. Hillary glanced at her own cup, still full to the top, but didn't want to reach for it and chance interrupting Maggie's story.

"The depression hit and there was no work at all." Maggie stared at the wall behind Hillary's head as if looking into an invisible past. "Patrick said he scrounged up odd jobs doing just about anything. That was when he knew he had the heart of a businessman, even called himself the Broome Company." Maggie laughed in a sort of whinny. "But he barely kept body and soul together. Looked out for his sister, Fianna. She kept the business parts straight and got taken along to work any job that called for more than one person. Well, it's clear he was smart and had a knack for fixing and building. Had the gift of gab, too. He could talk people into adding on an extra room or even a garage. He was a real charmer, up to the end. Teddy took after him in that way." Maggie's eyes welled up.

"By the end of the thirties, he'd bought a couple rundown properties inland in the Central Valley and set up his business in a garage, just before the Japs bombed Pearl Harbor." Hillary was unnerved to hear her use that slur.

"After that, he got a couple war contracts with the Navy down in Martinez. Money started coming in. But just when he needed his sister most, keeping his books and all the inventory organized, she up and ran off back to Ireland. That James boyfriend was home with an injury from fighting over in France. All's he had to do was crook his finger and Fianna ran off.

"Patrick was furious, vowed never to have women working in his company again. Well, that's the part . . ." Hillary could feel Maggie staring at her. She looked up from her notepad and waited. " . . . that's the part we don't want published, hear? That's the part that led to him making up that trust, keeping all the power in the men's hands—can't trust a woman with business." Maggie sat staring with hard eyes at Hillary, shaking her head.

"What happened after that?" Hillary asked. It was getting dark outside. "How did the family get started?" Maggie stood and took a wrought iron poker from the caddy, opened the fireplace screen, and began stabbing at logs, setting loose a flurry of hot embers.

"Well, Patrick got involved with the church here and met Eleanor. Married her in a hurry and your father"—Maggie glared at Hillary as if it were her fault—"was born after the war. Then John and Robert came along soon after, but that was the end of babies for Eleanor. Female troubles was all Patrick would say. Damn female troubles." Maggie shook her head and scowled.

"From the start, your father wanted to sit inside and read books, draw pictures, and listen to the radio. I think John might have been drawn that way a little, too. But not my Robert." Maggie grinned. "Robert was out in the shop all the time, trying to get into things. Stowed himself away at age three in a carpenter's truck to get to a job site." Maggie stood and laughed. "Grandad Pat, that's what we called him later on, he told that story over and over. 'Can't keep Robert off the job!' Loved that story." Maggie fell silent.

"Okay," Hillary said. She set her notepad down. "So my father was the bookworm and Uncle Robert was the builder. I got that part. How did you come into the picture?" Hillary checked to be sure the digital recorder was still on.

"My dad was one of Broome's carpenters. I would ride along in the truck sometimes, sit and color during the day as he worked. I was too young for school. My mother didn't want to be bothered." Maggie squeezed her eyes shut and went on with them closed, as if talking in her sleep. "She ended up drinking herself to death, and fast. Robert as a kid was always there at the worksites, too. We just fit together, a couple of misfits, we would laugh. All the way to the bank, as it turned out." Maggie gave a gentle snort.

"And now, Violet, that little vixen, she wants to take it all. She doesn't deserve it. I never wanted girls, anyway." Her voice became agitated. "She doesn't have a drop of business blood like her father and brother." Maggie picked up the brass bell and shook it in rhythm with her words. "Grandad Pat wouldn't a stood for it." Hillary was prepared for it but still found it shocking to hear Maggie talk about her own daughter like that.

"Remember that silver lining I told you about?" She let out a horsey bray. "I've got plenty of clout with adoption agencies. I'm going to stop Violet from keeping BC for herself." Her voice notched up to a shrill cry. "Don't have any sons by blood anymore, got to adopt. Grandad Pat . . ." She stared up at the painting of her men, dominating the room. "—all three of them. They want me to!" She rang the bell again and set it down with a bang on the end table.

Hillary was speechless at her vehemence. The housekeeper edged into the room, with her head bowed.

"Fresh coffee, Luisa," Maggie said, gesturing to her empty cup. "I'm surprised I had to ring."

"Mrs. Broome," the woman said. "I been hearing." She spoke so softly Hillary could barely make out her meaning.

"What do you mean?" Maggie stood and walked close to the fire. She picked up a poker.

"You need boy, son of Robert?" Luisa's eyes were open so wide they seemed to protrude.

"You've been out there listening to us?" Maggie turned, her jaw clenched, the poker stuck out at an odd angle.

"Just been in the hall a minute, Mrs. Broome. Just hear you say you need son."

"What? What do you mean?"

"Robert, he have one more son."

"What are you talking about?" Maggie scowled and put the poker back in its caddy.

"He always say never tell, but now . . ." Luisa rolled her apron ties between her fingers, making the ends flop back and forth. "Now Mr. Robert pass . . ." She tapped herself four times quickly with the sign of the cross.

Maggie stepped close to Luisa and clasped her shoulders. "What are you trying to say?"

"Mr. Robert, he make me do it, not tell you." A tear rolled down Luisa's cheek.

Maggie whirled to face Hillary. "Turn off that recorder. Now!"

Hillary felt stunned, almost paralyzed with what the housekeeper seemed to be saying. Maggie dashed to the coffee table. Picking up the recorder, she poked at it. "How do you shut the damn thing off? It's time for you to go."

Luisa started crying. "I'm sorry, Mrs. Broome. Angel is a good boy. Robert always provide for him."

"Get out of here," Maggie said, glaring at Hillary. "Now."

"He's a good boy." Luisa was sobbing. "He stay alone after school and never done a wrong thing."

Maggie turned back to Luisa. "How old is he?"

"Seventeen. A big boy. On the basketball team. He's a good boy." Luisa was smiling through her tears. "You would like my Angel, Robert's Angel."

"Angel Ramirez?" Maggie whispered.

"Angel Broome Ramirez," Luisa laughed. "Robert want to call him that."

Maggie turned to Hillary. "Go now. Do not mention this to anyone."

Hillary picked up her things from the coffee table. She turned to say good-bye but Maggie had her arm around Luisa's waist and was leading her from the room.

Hillary let herself out. The white picket gate opened automatically and closed behind her slowly. She raced across the dark street, icy rain pelting her exposed hands and cheeks. Rolls of thunder boomed across the sky.

Inside her car, Hillary's thoughts shot through her head like lightening bolts.

What a horrible mother Maggie was. A tiny woman of iron. Poor Violet. She had it worse than I did. At least my father believed in me. Neither of Violet's parents were there for her. *Better to be abandoned than have a witchy woman like Maggie scheming to keep me out of the picture. How will this Angel boy change things?*

Feeling a surge of sympathy for her cousin and knowing a newfound son could turn her world upside down, Hillary made up her mind to tell Violet about the love child. Angel. What a name.

ELEVEN

Violet

I WOKE FEELING APPREHENSIVE. *Would I be respected in my new position at Broome Construction?* I needed to show up in a "mantle of authority," as I'd heard suit jackets called. Yet I couldn't look too harsh. Grandad Pat never even wore a tie, but Dad had raised the company culture to a new level. The inside staff dressed in business styles, but of course that didn't apply to the shop and construction folks. I settled on a charcoal pinstriped suit with a raspberry silk ruffle cascading down the front.

Buddy caught me checking myself out in the hall mirror, all tense with my serious face on. "Hey, boss lady," he said, and slid his hands up under my jacket to tickle my sides. "Lighten up."

I doubled over laughing, and yelled for him to stop. *How was I so lucky have a man like him who could pass the partner test every time?*

We left the house in our separate cars, waving as we diverged at Highway 99, he north for his Sacramento office day, me over to Broome's complex west of Interstate 5.

* * *

Kaylyn greeted me in the lobby. "Coffee?"

I nodded. "Please, with nonfat milk." Down the hall, the double doors to Dad's office stood closed. Of course, I'd been in there before. Usually, though, he'd show up unexpected at my corner office in the accounting department. Or sometimes I'd be included in the conference room at the other end of the building. Teddy's office was out in the main warehouse in back. Dad's was understood to be off limits, more a place for good ol' boys doing their wheeling and dealing. Or that was my sense of it—I knew there was so much I had to learn.

Sucking in my breath, I pushed through both doors and stood at the edge of the dark brown carpet. Teddy had used this office last week after Dad died. Now here I was, the third person in less than two weeks to be running BC's planning and operations. Everything really. I hoped my tenure would last until I could turn over the reins to my son. The one Buddy and I were working on.

I surveyed Dad's office, about four times the size of mine. Through a plate glass window was an atrium, complete with grape varieties that did well in the San Joaquin Valley, now bare vines in their winter dormancy.

Dad's desk took a prominent position in the center of the room. His chair, a black leather affair with a brown and white hairhide back, was pushed up tight to the desk, as if guarding it from interlopers.

I sat in one of the black velour barrel chairs across from Dad's desk. The same chair I'd sat in that time I asked him if he would teach me the business. He'd started chuckling, and said I was good at my job, top notch with my degree in Accounting. He never answered my question, just took me out to lunch that afternoon. So humiliating. I'd never told anyone. I looked over at Dad's chair. *Got to stop calling it Dad's. It's mine now.*

Kaylyn carried in a tray sporting a mug of coffee with a glass pitcher of pale skim milk alongside. She looked at me and then across at Dad's chair, apparently confused as to whether I was the boss or not.

I stood and circled behind the desk, trying not to struggle as I pulled the heavy chair out. Sitting in its massive enclosure for the first time, I felt like Alice in Wonderland, having eaten from the cake that made her too tiny for the furniture.

Kaylyn smiled and leaned to place the coffee on the gold-tooled leather desk blotter. "Anything else?"

"Thanks, no. I want to get some of these things moved out to storage." I waved my hand in the air and then poured milk into my coffee, watching the white cloud form in the inky liquid. "Guess I can call out to the shop to get help, yes?" I looked at her.

"Sure. I can get them on the line for you." She nodded toward the chunky black phone on Dad's desktop. The desktop. *My* desktop.

"It's okay. I need to think it over first." I blew on my coffee and took a sip. "Actually, what's the name of that woman who stages our models?"

"Donna. Donna Lister. She's done all the BC homes for the past couple of years." Kaylyn took the phone in hand.

It was amazing to watch her in action. I could see how addictive it might be, to have someone do little things like this for me. She punched numbers into the phone, listened, and spoke in cheery, firm tones. "Good morning. Ms. Violet Broome would like a word with you." She handed the phone to me, smiled brightly, and left the office.

"Hi," I said. "I wondered if you might come help me decide what to do with my father's office. It's just so . . ." What? What was it that did not fit? "So massive. You know?" My voice sounded thin and high.

Donna said she'd be over in an hour to run some preliminary ideas past me. I hung up and walked the perimeter of the office. Bookshelves on one wall held photos of housing development projects all over the country. Grandad Pat took center stage in many of them, cheerful grin below his BC hardhat. An Old West-style bar, stocked with booze of all kinds, ran along the opposite wall. Completing the big box of a room was the window wall overlooking the atrium.

Everything done in black, brown, and white. Should I grow myself into this masculine scheme? I never knew if this really fit Teddy either—my brother who'd dreamed of becoming a baseball player.

The intercom buzzed and took my mind off Teddy. It was Kaylyn with a request to meet with BC's mortgage bankers this afternoon. I agreed to see Jake Mortenson and Larry Wagner and start learning how to network among the good-ol'-boys. I hadn't been allowed in with them much. Teddy hadn't either, but not because Dad didn't try to rope him in. Teddy just preferred to hang out with the carpenters and organize Broome softball teams up and down the valley. He loved being one of the blue collar guys, having a good time. He'd seemed happy in that last week of his life, starting to make deals. Maybe he was learning to play ball in a new way.

At least I was stepping into the job knowing how some of the numbers added up. Along with so many other businesses lately, our bottom line had been growing. It felt like we were swelling faster and faster as we neared the end of 2005. I sometimes got the image of an Italian accordion player, with his squeeze box pulled out to its widest.

Kaylyn buzzed me that Donna Lister was here and I told her to send her in. I was surprised to realize Donna was the blonde who'd been rebuffed by Teddy at the burial. But neither of us mentioned the funeral and I warmed up to her as she laid out three preliminary proposals she'd constructed for me and started introducing each of them.

"First, we have a similar look to your father's but scaled back, sort of a cowgirl-makes-good look. Lots of brown leather but also blue denim and bright orange silk touches. The bar is replaced by a wine bar, the hairhide chair backs replaced by burlap. Photos of yangy women on the walls, like *Annie Get your Gun* posters."

I was intrigued.

"Next, a sort of Central Valley theme, lots of images of the main crops—grapes, corn, asparagus, cherries. In shades of green, yellow, red—a harvest feeling, earthy, rich, fecund." I thought of the baby that might be forming right now in my belly. Fecund. Great word.

"Plows, farm implements, barns, and so on." Donna smiled brightly, her white teeth glistening.

The last package she set out was in shades of purple and gold.

"This plan conveys a sort of regal ambiance. Strong and rich like Broome homes themselves. Impressive." She fingered fabric swatches cut out with zigzag edges, laid in sets of three shades for each color. "We have just a touch of purple's complementary color, as well, to keep things fresh. Needless to say, we subtly weave in your first name with the notion of royal power and authority."

I was charmed. In high school, I had learned my name's meaning and liked it. A "violet room" felt like an infusion of self-esteem and somehow a weird confirmation that with the gift of my name, my parents might have felt a sweet confidence in me. Back then.

What a strange new day. New in so many ways. Or potentially new. I felt just this side of being overwhelmed. Donna spoke softly. "Teddy would like any of these for you. He spoke so highly of you."

She called him Teddy. Like I did. I felt like crying. My love for him had been so mixed with envy all these years. I told Donna I would think over her ideas and get back to her.

* * *

The phone rang and it was Hillary's fiancé, Ed. He wanted to come talk to me. He agreed to wait and come tomorrow. I hung up, feeling anxious. Why was the law interested in me?

I opened Dad's top desk drawer and wasn't surprised to find it super tidy. In one of the little compartments was his key to what he'd called the executive washroom—Dad had made a joke of it but everyone knew it mattered.

The discreet sign on the hallway door read MEN. I would no longer be relegated to the WOMEN's room. A warmth swelled through my body. I turned the key and walked in. The décor was so much like Dad's office—all black, brown, and white with leather horse tackle for towel racks.

I washed my face and combed my hair into a soft bun, put on fresh lipstick, and gave myself a talking to in the mirror. Had to look good for the bankers visit this afternoon. Why had Teddy been so hostile to them, two of Dad's best buds?

Kaylyn sent out for a small salad for me, and I ate alone in my huge new office, pouring over spreadsheets trying to understand more about who was connected to the numbers and how.

At two, Jake Mortenson arrived with his partner Larry Wagner in tow.

When Kaylyn ushered them in, I stood and nodded across the big desk, glad for a second that the room was still outfitted in the power icons of my father. "Good to see you, gentlemen," I said and gestured for them to sit in the barrel chairs across from me.

They looked so serious. "We're sorry about your recent losses," said Larry.

"We wanted to get to know you better," Jake added. "Of course we know you as part of the family, but now . . ."

"Yes," I said. "I'm going to need a lot of help to keep the company running smoothly after losing Dad and Teddy in such quick succession." I felt like I was saying the lines from a movie script, some kind of melodrama. *Push on.*

The two men nodded and sat silent. I was on stage. They were testing me. I could feel it. Almost like an interview at which I would either get hired and win or be passed over and lose. What should I say to them?

"I'd like to keep our relationship going same as before," I said, watching to see their reactions. Nothing yet.

"As you know, I've been the company's accounting

officer for years, so I know the numbers, the bottom line." Their faces brightened.

"What I need from you"—I could feel the power shifting in the room—"is to just keep on keeping on." I laughed. "How can we argue with success?"

"Sky's the limit," boomed Jake, flashing me a grin. "Good thing you see how important it is for us locals here to offer everyone the chance at the American Dream. Not just traditional buyers anymore." He stood. "I couldn't understand why your brother was trying to bring in outsiders. He was too influenced by his friends in the sports world."

Jake walked over to Dad's bar and turned to me. "Glad to see you are your father's daughter." He laughed and gestured toward the bar. "Mind?"

"Please." I waved toward the array of bottles. He poured a whiskey neat for himself, one for Larry and one for me. Some women might have been insulted but I needed to become buddies with these boys.

I forced myself not to choke on the powerful drink.

Kaylyn buzzed and asked if I would take a call from Hillary Broome. "She says it's important."

I picked up the phone and told Hillary I was busy at the moment, but I'd call her later.

The men joked about their golf scores and asked if I played. I told them I was taking lessons—not really a lie since I now planned to.

We set up a golf date for next week, out at the Country Club. I'd have to get Buddy to take me around the course right away.

* * *

I took home a briefcase of papers, but this time concentrated on learning more about the people who ran the
company and our deeper connections to other businesses. Not just on paper, as I was used to seeing them
on spreadsheets, but who they were as human beings.
Tonight Buddy was working late up in Sacramento.

My evening started with leftover spaghetti and a
touch of Zinfandel. Then I spread out papers on the dining room table. All right. Donna was in charge of the
interior designs, in both the residential and the new com-
mercial ventures we were hoping to get into. Amazing for
one so young. Was there more to her connection to the
company than just business? I'd have to talk to her about
that some time.

There were the investment brokers Dad had been
seeing lately. I studied the paperwork. A visual of the ac-
tivities might help. I got out my laptop and opened up
Word's graphing tool. Rain pattered against the dark
window glass.

I stood and started a fire. Sitting down, I flipped the
pages back to the early 1990s and began tracking the
number of loans Broome Company was handling on behalf of our buyers. An hour passed and I was still en-
grossed with my numbers, those safe havens that allowed
for a momentary illusion that life all made sense, that
there was some kind of rational bottom line, devoid of
messy emotional traps.

I jumped a fraction of an inch off my chair as the

door from the garage banged open and Buddy walked in, booming a greeting.

"You scared me!" I stood and hugged myself, rubbing my upper arms. "Wow, I got lost in my numbers."

"Did two and two add up to four?" He laughed and walked over to give me a hug.

"It is looking incredible, the upswing in the amount of loan money moving through the business over time," I said, pointing to my laptop screen.

A jagged line started at one million back in 1990 and now, in 2005, fifteen years later, we were closing in on three billion dollars in loans instigated by Broome Corporation. "That's a massive mountain of growth. Not sure what to make of it."

Buddy studied it a few seconds and gave a low whistle. "Must be why my bundled mortgages are doing so well. Who was your dad working with to get all that much dough flowing?"

"I know some of them," I said. "Next on my agenda is to try and meet more of them face to face. Learn what's happening, what the plans are for the future. Got to get with our legal department, too. Look into our contracts." I sighed. "A couple bankers came by this afternoon, Mortenson and Wagner. Got to learn to fit in, be one of the guys myself."

"That'll be the day." Buddy poured himself a whiskey and looked over at me with a question in his eyes.

"Sure, I'll have one. I'm practicing that part of being a good ol' boy." I laughed and put away my work for the night. I'd forgotten to call Hillary and now it was too late. I'd call tomorrow. My tomorrows stretched out in a glittering line of hopes and dreams, with fears pushed off to the side of the highway.

TWELVE

Ed

ED AND WALT DROVE OUT to Broome Construction headquarters and were escorted by a friendly receptionist to Violet Broome's office. Ed looked around at the space and whistled. "You got big boots to fill here, lady." He felt oddly close to this cousin of Hillary's. With her brother out of the picture, he wondered how Violet would fare. And what her real feelings were toward her brother.

Violet waved them to matching barrel chairs facing her desk. Dressed in a white wool suit, she frowned and placed both hands on the desk, palms down. "How can I help you?" She drummed her fingers flat on the tooled leather desk blotter.

"What did you notice Saturday, before Ted collapsed?" Ed started to feel uncomfortable. "Sorry about your loss," he added.

Violet's head dropped for a second and she lifted a hand to her forehead. "It was horrible." She gazed at her desk for a few seconds, and with an index finger began tracing the gold pattern embossed in the blotter.

"You were there." She looked up, her eyes welling with tears. "You saw how awful it was. One minute, Teddy was the life of the party. Next minute, on the floor, dying." She pulled open a desk drawer and drew out some tissues.

Walt looked around the room, coughed, and pulled out his big white handkerchief to wipe his mouth.

Ed waited a few seconds before going on. "Can you tell us what you did that morning? Before and after the service, up to when Ted stood to confront that man."

"Me?" She pressed tissues to the corners of her eyes. Ed noticed they were gray like Hillary's. Must run in the family—cousins. Mary Beth's eyes had been gray. He sighed and nodded at Violet.

"You want to know what I did?"

"It's just standard procedure, not to worry." Ed felt on the guilty side. It was almost a lie. She'd had so much to gain from Ted's death.

"Well," she said. "I was in the kitchen at first, helping Jojo." She looked Ed straight in the eyes. "That's what I call Joanna. We've run around together since we were kids."

Ed nodded.

"Okay, so Jojo had this new recipe for goulash. Her husband is Czech, you know? They're off to Europe to pick up ideas for the restaurant." She looked away, as if wishing she were somewhere else.

He nodded at her to continue. *How is this shrinking violet going to take on the sharks in the corporate world BC operates in?*

"Okay, so I was back in the kitchen at first, making sure the food was all being kept at the right temperature. Didn't want anyone getting sick." She stared at Ed with wide eyes.

She looked like a black lab puppy, begging silently for a biscuit, Ed thought.

"Then I went out to find Teddy."

Ed noted she called him Teddy, as had Donna. Not Ted or Theodore, like most everyone else.

The corners of her mouth turned down. "He was late, as usual." She kept a handful of tissues wadded in her fist.

"Late," she repeated. "I used to tease that he would be late to his own funeral and he'd just laugh about it! And say 'Good!'" Tears spilled from her eyes.

Ed wondered if she was sincere or just a good actress. He felt he was torturing Hillary's cousin and not even sure yet if this was a homicide. "I'm sorry to put you through this, Violet. We can come back later. Maybe next week?"

Violet nodded into her tissues. Ed walked behind the desk and patted her on the shoulder. "I'll phone you in a day or two."

She looked up at him with a faint smile. "Thank you, Ed." She sniffed and lowered her face down onto her wad of tissues.

Ed and Walt left the building. Out in the car, they looked at each other, grim-faced. "Not sure what to make of her," Ed said. "I feel bad since we don't even know if we've got a homicide or not. The autopsy showed he didn't choke to death though. That tox lab is too damn slow."

Walt flashed a rare smile. "The bright side is we're going to get out of town soon. Get up to Reno for that hotel buffet." Walt pursed his lips together.

Ed laughed. "They advertise they never met an appetite they can't conquer. A final fling before your New Year's resolution kicks in?"

"I never said I'd go on any diet, partner." Walt scowled.

"Better think about it," Ed said. "Let me call Hillary. See how she's coming—make sure my bride hasn't changed her mind." He laughed at his own joke. She was a woman he felt he could trust.

THIRTEEN

Hillary

HILLARY WAS EAGER to meet with Violet, in sympathy for what she might face when she heard about Angel. It was not the kind of thing you told someone on the phone. She had to wait for Violet to call her back. Hillary felt close to Violet now. It was really worse to have an evil mother than an absent one. She knew she'd get a call right away if they were sisters instead of cousins though.

Roger had stayed over in San Francisco so she couldn't run this shocking news by him. It was both flattering and irritating that he'd begun relying heavily on her to keep The Acorn going while he was off working on Gay Pride issues in the city. Mildred, their volunteer receptionist, left at noon to meet her friend Sarah Stoney for their weekly hospital volunteer work.

Hillary had never been able to make friends well. Even before her mother ran off and abandoned her, Hillary had been shy—a bookworm like her father, lost in a fantasy world. Last month, she'd met Sarah and felt a strong connection to the motherly widow. So strong that Hillary had worked up enough courage to rescue Sarah from a madman and save her life. Hillary'd enjoyed the times she'd met Sarah since then for lunch at Little Joe's Café. She phoned Sarah and left a voice mail to set up lunch plans.

Hillary sat alone at the newspaper office, acutely aware of how isolated she was when compared to the others in the lively Broome family. Work and school had been her major social life, but they were wearing thin. She was eager to meet Ed later for dinner.

Learning about Robert Broome's love child had changed Hillary's mind about writing a feature focused on Broome Construction. She wanted to widen her scope, find out more about developers in general, what kind of people they were.

The man with the sign going berserk at the funeral reception had been protesting mold infestation in his BC house. Hillary searched reliable websites and found many cases of people discovering black mold in their walls and air conditioning systems. A few babies had even contracted fatal lung infections. An upsurge of litigation in the early twenty-first century had forced most insurance companies to exclude mold from coverage. Her reporter's instinct suggested it was conceivable the protestor had sprayed something into the air that caused Ted to choke. Not likely but possible.

Hillary drove out to The Vineyards, one of several of BC's housing projects near Lodi. In the winter weather, the model homes looked sad, their landscaping bedraggled. However, bright BC flags and signs welcomed homebuyers, and the small lot next to the models was more than half full of cars on this weekday. Hillary threaded her way along the footpath, set up to funnel people into the sales office, a converted triple garage of the largest home among the four models.

She was greeted by a man in a navy suit wearing a tie dotted with tiny BC logos.

"Welcome," he said. "Make yourself at home. I'm here if you have any questions."

"I'd like to just go through the houses now." She and Ed might want to buy a house after they got married, and she knew she could get more information if she came across as a buyer more so than as a reporter.

"Of course, enjoy!" He handed her a packet filled with floor plans and lists of amenities. "These are an excellent value in today's market—not many lots left. Almost sold out here and ready to open our new release in the spring. These prices are locked in until the end of December. Kind of a holiday gift." He flashed a brilliant smile, as if on TV, advertising teeth whitener strips. "We offer financial packages to fit every buyer's needs."

The first house had a charming nursery. The longing

for her own family grew stronger day by day. She worried she still didn't know how Ed felt about this. Was it a mistake to run off to Reno so soon? She'd have to have a frank talk with him at dinner tonight.

After she finished her tour, Hillary sat at the salesman's desk. "My fiancé and I are looking around for a place," she said, unwrapping a Hershey's kiss from a glass jar decorated with hearts drawn around BC logos.

He tilted back in his ergonomic chair. "When is your special day?"

"Well, we haven't exactly set it yet." She twiddled the ring Ed had given her on Thanksgiving. "But it could be soon, when I'm on semester break."

"You're a teacher?" He gave her a thumbs-up. "My sister's a teacher. Wonderful people."

"I work part-time at Clearwater College." She didn't want to reveal she was a journalist or this man wasn't likely to give her the information she was here for.

"Do you have any homeowners I can talk to and see how they like living in their homes? How the floor plan worked out for them?"

"Pardon?"

"You know, testimonials?" Her heart was pounding so hard she thought he might be able to hear it.

"Oh. A list of satisfied homeowners." He frowned.

"I wouldn't want to take such a serious step without talking to anyone really living there." She bent forward to stand up. He wasn't going to be any help.

"We've got client testimonials up now on our new website. Have you seen it?"

"My fiancé would want to talk to people right around here." She stood.

"Wait a second." He rummaged around in a bottom drawer and fished out a rumpled sheet of paper. Eight or ten short statements were listed, names below each, but no addresses. "These are from buyers in our older Northern California projects."

She reached out and took the paper. It's a start.

Thanking him, she left before he changed his mind. The names were like finding gold in her search. She would teach the students how to get folks to interview. That man running crazy through the parish hall with his big sign could have had something to do with Ted's death. And he must have lived in some established development, for mold to have time to get a foothold.

* * *

She got to school by midafternoon. The student journalists were busy on their projects, as usual. These young people loved learning this business. Daniel, the editor-in-chief this fall, looked up as she came into their room, outfitted with newsroom style desks instead of the typical tablet arm seats in a classroom.

She laid the handout of satisfied homeowners flat on Daniel's desk. "Want to help me get interviews on a possible homicide?" Three other bright-eyed student writers gathered around.

"Okay, we've got eight names here. What we need are their addresses and phone numbers. She cut the handout into four strips and passed a strip to each student. "Take these and first try the reverse phone book. Then if that doesn't work, see what else you can think of."

Hillary watched them flip through various phone books the newsroom kept for locations in the Central Valley. She sat at her desk, feeling satisfied over their energy and work ethic. These were great kids. Would she ever have any kids of her own?

* * *

"Hillary!" She had the students call her by her first name, the way an editor and staffers do in a real newspaper office.

She nodded at Natalie, one of the smartest in the class.

"I just talked to a homeowner. He said we could interview him." Natalie's brown eyes sparkled as she handed over her slip of paper with a phone number and address jotted next to one of the testimonials. Natalie had a lot of promise. She was a natural as a poet and strung words together effortlessly in her stories as well.

"James Z. Townsend," Hillary read aloud from the strip of paper. She recognized the address as being in a high-end development at the edge of Lodi. One that had been around for five years or so. "Did he say when?"

"Anytime tonight, after five thirty."

The wall clock's little hand was nearly at five. Hillary needed to stop for gas on the way so they had to hurry. "Come on then, Natalie." It was dark already as the two of them walked out to the parking lot and got into Hillary's car. She turned her heater on high to warm them up fast.

Hillary filled up at Arco, frowning at paying nearly $3.00 a gallon, and grateful her little VW Golf was so fuel-efficient.

She found her way quickly but before she could get to Townsend's house, she was stopped by a brightly lit gated entry next to a sign announcing Broome Acres. Waiting until a car drove out, she sped in before the gate closed. Her little car was great for things like that. She drove by tall date palms lining the streets.

They looked nothing like the native oaks, sycamores, and wild grapes that still grew alongside the creeks and roads. Hillary wondered what it had all looked like in the days before any white man stepped on this land. It would make a good story project for the students if things in town ever calmed back down enough for the blessing of boredom.

"Do you live in a place like this?" Hillary asked Natalie as they drove along the curved wide street, looking for Townsend's address.

"No, ma'am." Natalie wrinkled her nose. "I'm from South Stockton, went to Ford High School. Don't know anyone who lives in these fancy places."

Hillary slowed the car. Luckily, most of the houses had plenty of outdoor lighting. When they got near the number they were looking for, they found it was one of the few that looked dark. Was this guy really home?

"Come on." Hillary got out of the car, grateful she

had brought Natalie along. The dark house broadcast a spooky feeling, as if this were Halloween. She felt like a little kid, hoping for no tricks tonight.

Hillary rang the bell, outlined faintly by a slim circle of light. Winchester chimes rang out on the quiet street. They waited on the porch for someone to answer but no one came. "Are you sure this is the right address?" Hillary asked.

Natalie's shoulders slumped. They stared at each other. Hillary rang the doorbell again.

Without warning, the door opened wide. A tall thin man stood inside, holding a sleeping baby and scowling at them, dark circles under his eyes.

"Shhhhhhh," he mouthed and rolled his head in a gesture for them to come in. Hillary stepped gingerly into the dim entry, tiled with black marble, followed by Natalie. The man nodded toward a light in the back of the house. He nodded again, then disappeared down a hall to the left.

Hillary and Natalie walked toward the light and found themselves in a great room, a combo kitchen and family room space. Hillary walked around the kitchen, noticing an empty baby bottle and a jar of baby food at the table, the jar half full of what must have been apricots, going by the label.

The man walked into the kitchen. "Sorry," he whispered. "You came a bit early. Had to get Christopher to sleep. Have a seat." He reached over to turn on a baby monitor and adjusted the sound so they could just hear a soft snoring coming from the speaker.

"Damn mold. Don't think it's normal for a baby to snore, do you?" He sat at the table, without clearing the baby food dishes. Just then a beeper sounded, and he rose again to open the oven door, take out a TV dinner and set it on the stovetop.

Now that she'd had time to get a look at him, Hillary knew he was not the same man who'd run through the parish hall. It was such a long shot anyway. "Sorry. Don't know much about babies, but thanks for agreeing to talk to us. My name's Hillary Broome," she said and hurried to add, ". . . but I'm only a distant relation to the folks who built this development."

The man sat and clenched his jaw. "Are you now?" He glared at her, shifting his dark eyes back and forth between her and Natalie. "And who is this young lady?"

"I'm the student who called you, sir." It was a good thing Natalie had come along if they were going to get anything out of this man, thought Hillary. She looked so fresh-faced and earnest. "From the college paper."

He nodded his head and sighed. "You're looking for testimonials for the houses, right?"

Hillary nodded along with him. "Really, we want to find the man who showed up at Robert Broome's funeral and then ran through the reception later. He had a sign protesting Broome Homes, the mold issues. Have you heard of anyone like that?"

He pursed his lips and nodded. "Hmmmmm. I'd like to find him myself, and join in. Damn insurance company won't let us sue. What the hell are we supposed to do?"

He walked to the stove and lifted an aluminum cover off his TV dinner. "How did you get my name?" Without waiting for a response, he set his food on the table and yanked a fork from a nearby drawer, glancing up at the ceiling as he slammed shut the drawer.

"Just have to pray no spores are drifting down onto our silverware. Damn them to hell and back."

He sat and began forking apart what looked like some kind of meat patty. Hillary couldn't tell in the dim light.

"Damn who?" Hillary set the straps of her tote bag over the back of her chair. It looked like the man was going to cooperate.

"That Robert Broome and those S.O.B.s who work for him." He dug into a flattened mound of potatoes halfway covering the meat. "How'd you find me?"

"The salesman at the model homes had your name on a list of testimonials," she said.

He sat chewing silently, swallowed, then spat out his words. "Those greedy bastards! Got my remarks right after we moved in, when things looked on the up and up for the wife and me." He glared at Hillary as if his troubles were her fault. A sound of the baby fussing came over the monitor speaker. "Never get any rest now. Can't hardly control little Chris's asthma. Got to go." He stood up and headed out of the room.

"Can we phone you later?" Hillary called after him.

He turned to nod sharply and disappeared down the hall as the baby monitor delivered a cascade of hoarse, breathy cries.

"Let's get out of here," Hillary said, and grabbed her tote, nodding at Natalie. They retraced their steps back out front and settled into the car.

"Wow," said Natalie. "That guy's got a pile of trouble."

"Doesn't look good. Spores dropping from the ceiling? Where's his wife? I want to see if I can get other homeowners to talk." By the time Hillary got Natalie back to her car, it was seven thirty.

After she watched her student drive off, she phoned Ed from her cell to make sure they were still on for dinner. He'd been working late, too, and they firmed up plans to meet at Don Luis' Mexican Restaurant just off Highway 99 near her Morada cottage. The place had become a favorite with Hillary.

* * *

He'd arrived before her and was nursing a Dos Equis. His lean face just hinting at middle-aged jowls brought to her mind a tired and lovable bloodhound.

He rose to enfold her in his arms. Their waitress was standing nearby with a grin on her face. "Pajaros del amor," she sang out. "Lovebirds!"

Hillary blushed and clung to Ed until he held her out at arms' distance.

"Sit down and relax. Beer?" He pulled out a chair for her.

Ed didn't know she wasn't a beer drinker. In fact, she hated it. She hoped they didn't run into serious trouble over what they still had to learn about each other. She'd jumped in too soon with Tom, got engaged before she knew about his need to blame women for his dysfunction. Ugh. Then with Charles. How could she not have seen he was just using her for her father's connections?

"Dos Equis?" Ed was holding up the bottle as if in a TV ad.

She shook her head. "No thanks, I don't like beer." He must have assumed she drank the occasional beer. Her heart skipped a beat. She was going to have to bring up the topic of children. Tonight.

Alicia, her favorite server at the family-run restaurant, nodded in recognition when Hillary asked for a local Zinfandel.

"Any update on Ted's autopsy?" Hillary sat down across from Ed. "It would help to know how to investigate for the story."

Ed shook his head. "Nada. Still waiting on whether it was a natural death or homicide." He sighed. "But I do have some news for you."

She took her glass of wine from Alicia and clinked it against his beer bottle. "What's that?" She swirled the wine gently, inhaled its aroma, and took a sip, rolling the wine around in her mouth to bring out the flavor.

"I talked Walt into coming along to Reno with us, got him to agree to be best man when we run off like lovestruck teenagers." His voice was pitched high with enthusiasm.

"Yikes!" She set down her wine and lifted a bottle of

hot sauce off the table. She picked at the label to mask her shock.

"Yikes?" He frowned and bent forward.

"I assumed it would just be the two of us." She could feel her face heating up. "You know those chapels, the people who run them act as witnesses, don't they?" He must not have realized she didn't have anyone to ask to stand up with her.

"I just thought we would be bringing along a couple friends. Guess we don't have to, though. Sorry." He pursed his lips, his frown deepened.

Hillary drained her wine and glared at him. "You didn't know I hate beer and didn't know that I don't have anyone to ask to be a bridesmaid. We don't really know each other, do we?"

"It's not a big deal," Ed said. "Walt won't mind not going--he's not such a fan of weddings anyway. Since his wife died, he likes not having any responsibility the way he did when he had to take care of her."

Alicia poured Hillary another glass of wine and left the bottle on the table.

"Marriage," Hillary said. "Walt's glad he's out of it, and I know almost nothing about it. Frankly . . ." She took another swallow of wine. "It scares me. You haven't told me any details about your marriage—what happened?" Hillary shook her head no when Alicia came over with her order pad out. "Why haven't we even talked about it?"

"When everything started, it was fine." Ed finished off his beer and ordered another one. "It took a couple years for it to dawn on me that Elizabeth was in it for the security of being married to a cop." He cracked his neck and lifted his fresh beer to his lips.

Hillary felt a pang in her gut. She was looking to belong, for a family, for her own family. Belonging— how was that different from security?

"What's so bad about security?" she asked.

"How about some love thrown in, you know?" Ed scraped his fingers through his hair. "Some damn love. Is that too much too ask?"

"How do you know she didn't love you?" Hillary's heart raced and she held her breath a few long moments while Ed started coughing and got up, headed for the men's room.

Hillary poured herself the rest of the wine. She'd never had a whole bottle all on her own, not since she broke up with that weird Tom. That night, she'd jumped up out of bed and ran out of his apartment in her underwear, after she realized he was blaming his incompetence on her. She'd run down the stairs at midnight, jeans and tee shirt in her arms and jumped into her old Toyota Corolla, thankful she hadn't moved in with him and still had her own place.

She could feel her face burning and was grateful it was late so not many diners were still there. Alicia and the others puttered around cleaning up the kitchen. A sip at a time, she drank until Ed came back.

He sat and ran his the flat of his palms across the table top. "Shouldn't we talk this over more privately?"

"No. Let's get it out on the table. No sense in pussy

footing around." She laughed a horsy laugh, one she'd never heard come from her before. She felt strong enough to force the moment to a head. "So why did your marriage break up?" Ed stared across the table at her, with his long lean frowny face, that bloodhound look again. Didn't look so charming now.

"It's tied up with something else," he said. "It's hard to talk about."

"So that's why we've got to get it out--Holy Mary, we can't run off to Reno and set ourselves up for failure." She nodded and held up two fingers when Alicia waved a full coffee pot in their direction.

"Well," Ed said, "Elizabeth was a dutiful wife, but she was a great mother," he said. "Took our two girls everywhere--ballet, horseback riding, you name it. I loved them too, proud papa when Mary Beth wrote a letter to me for father's day--won first prize in the school contest. She was daddy's girl." He frowned and reached out for a cup of coffee as Alicia served them.

Hillary's heart softened. I knew it! He's got that good dad flavor about him. Just like my father. She leaned across the table and started to drew a heart on his face with her finger tip. He jerked his head away.

"That was when Mary Beth was seven. When she was ten," he gulped, "she sang a song in the school musical that cut my heart out, her voice was so pure and innocent. Puff the Magic Dragon, it was and from then on, we were inseparable. Mary Beth and me. She was practically our mascot down at the sheriffs. Elizabeth was jealous and tried every trick in the book to get Mary

Beth's attention away from me. When that didn't work, Elizabeth concentrated on keeping Caron and me as far apart as possible."

He rested his chin in his palms, elbows propped on the table, and spoke through clenched jaws, his lips barely moving. "Went on for years, happy. But she got to be a teenager, went out joy riding with her friends, in some of Stockton's rough neighborhoods." He sat straight up and drilled his next words straight at Hillary. "One night, I got the call. Hit and run. We never found the driver. Yet." His shoulders slumped.

"How awful." Hillary was stunned.

"Elizabeth blamed me. Took Caron and moved out to the East Coast with her family. Cut off all contact."

Hillary felt like she'd been punched in the gut.

Ed took her hands in his. "I've been a frozen man since then, five years now. But you've thawed me, Chick-adee. You and your Holy Mary." He smiled.

"But—but—" Hillary sputtered. "After that pain, how could you want another family? Take a chance again?"

Ed frowned. "I'm sure I want you, but not so sure about more kids."

"No kids?" She could barely hear herself whispering. "You don't want any children?" She felt hollow inside. "Not even with me?"

"In all honesty, I'm just not sure," he said.

"Okay. Red light," she said. "Time out. Let's put a halt to running off to Reno." She drained her coffee and stood. "I'm going home." She strode past Alicia and ran out into the dark parking lot.

Her body throbbed with a double dose of pain—her own and the hurt she knew she'd caused him. She loved him, she was certain. But she wasn't ready to face marriage. Not yet.

Maybe not ever.

FOURTEEN

Hillary

HILLARY TOOK A SLEEPING PILL when she got home, so she didn't have to think about Ed. But, she tossed in a sweat all night, dreaming of thrashing around under heavy fur coverings, in some kind of cave, strange men pressed up against her all night long. Outside the cave, babies cried. All night long.

The next morning, it took three cups of French Roast and a stinging hot shower before she felt the weight of the antique diamond ring. She pulled it off and walked around the cottage, waggling it back and forth, making the diamond dance like a jagged crystal ball. She put it to rest by slipping it over the hook by the front door where she hung her keys. It was a key in its own right but she wasn't sure what it unlocked.

Ed had left a string of voice mail messages but she wanted nothing more than to lose herself in work, put aside the fantasy of happily ever after with him. Or any man.

It hadn't worked out with Tom up in Sacramento. He'd asked her to marry him but never seemed to find time to get her an engagement ring. It took a couple years to realize he wanted to blame all his problems on her.

She'd sworn off men then. Until she got out east to Columbia and was wined and dined by the sophisticated Charles. But he was just out to use her for her father's connections with the LA Chronicle. Dropped her like a hot rock when the newspaper started trying to force their old-timers into golden handshakes, make them take early retirement.

It hurt that she didn't have anyone close enough to ask to stand up for her in a wedding but if Ed wasn't sure he wanted any more kids, that was even worse. *Holy Mary. What have I got myself into?*

She drove over to *The Acorn*. Roger was still not back. Some friend he was, not even an editor lately so busy in San Francisco preparing for next year's Gay Pride Parade. There was no one to help create a list of possible suspects if Ted's death turned out to be murder. All she had to work with was this Mold Man. And that was an impossible long shot.

Mildred had brought in homemade cinnamon rolls, and *The Acorn* office seemed as inviting a place as any.

Hillary pulled up her chair and gazed at the blank computer screen, tempted to Google stories on mold in housing developments, see what she might find to help build
her story. She got up and made a pot of French Roast in
the back room, resisting temptation, intent on getting
over that bad habit. But plagiarism was more than a bad
habit, really. Could cause the college to let her go and she
wasn't sure how long Roger would stand by her either.
Plagiarism was such a nasty accusation, but who in this
internet age didn't copy and paste once in a while? If she
were free to be honest, that topic would be perfect for a
story in its own right. Maybe someday she'd write a public mea culpa.

* * *

She turned her attention back to James, the man in
the dark house. She needed to learn what happened to
him, see if he might know more about the protestor from
the funeral than he was letting on.

It was weird how the real Mold Man had been allowed to hang around at Robert's burial. The cemetery
security was too unobtrusive, yet the courts were uphold-
ing free speech on funeral picketing, revolting as it
seemed. There was a story here, she knew. She called
James' number but got no answer.

She had to find that protestor. Might be too danger-
ous to take along student journalists. She decided to go
back out to the model homes, try to find more homeowners to contact.

In the garage-turned-sales-office, the same cheery man was waved Hillary into a chair. "Back again! We have just a couple beauties left in this release. Easy to qualify nowadays, too. What do you need?" He sat and pulled out a yellow legal pad, along with a pen inscribed "Broome Homes."

It was better to stay on the salesman's good side. "Well, I'm here as a reporter today. For *The Acorn*, the little weekly covering our region." She smiled as if to allay his fears of bad publicity. "We want to run a story on the housing boom and its positive impact on the local economy. I wonder if you have other contacts I could reach out to, you know like the ones you showed me yesterday?"

"Good timing," he said. "We just put out a new list." He pulled open a file drawer, drew a sheet out of a folder and handed it to her. "Here, contact any of these folks, get their word on how happy they are in their BC Homes."

Hillary took the flyer. "Appreciate it."

"Sure," he said, doodling circles on his yellow pad. "Sure. Those are better than the ones yesterday. More up-to-date and got the addresses and gate code, too."

They must have paid them for their endorsements.

* * *

She drove to the street of the first address on the list, in a development five miles or so from where she and Natalie had visited the day before. She got lucky and found about a third of the residents at home—a uniformly upbeat group. She wondered how much incentive BC was giving them for their word-of-mouth testimonials. It took her most of the afternoon. Kind of a good thing because it let her keep her phone turned off and ignore Ed's calls.

Not one of the homeowners had a bad word to say about the development, not even when asked specifically about mold issues. They had just been in those houses a few years, though, maybe not enough time for mold to grow.

She gave up there and drove back to the development where James lived, again after five in the evening. It was pitch dark. She rang his bell. No answer. She went next door and rang that bell, standing patiently on the covered porch, done in an Italian style. The door opened suddenly, flooding the porch with light.

"Yes?" A plump fortyish woman stood there, wooden spoon in hand, dripping some kind of pale batter, her other hand cupped below the spoon to catch the runoff.

Hillary introduced herself and explained she was trying to locate the man next door. "Do you have any idea when he might be home?"

"Oh, James, poor man. Come on in, dearie." She turned her head in the direction of her entry. Hillary stepped into the bright space and followed the woman through a great room into a large kitchen with a table set for six people.

"Sit." The woman plunged her spoon into a stainless

steel bowl and stirred vigorously, frowning. "I'm just about to fry up some ling cod. Hubby likes to go to the coast and catch it, you know. We freeze it for nights like this." She left the bowl sitting next to a restaurant-sized cooktop and walked to her stainless steel sink. "James. Sad story, that."

"I was hoping to get names of other homeowners with mold issues." Hillary began to feel hungry when she saw the woman lift thick pieces of white fish from the sink, set them on a cutting board, and slice them into long slim chunks. "Some who had something against Broome Construction Company."

"Well, James heard about the mold troubles in another BC development, a place near the Delta lowlands, too damp to build in, really. James took to walking our streets here, asking if we had checked our walls, ceilings, air-conditioning ducts and so forth." She looked up at the vent covers in her ceiling.

"And?" Hillary looked around the room trying to spot vent covers in the great room ceiling extending from the kitchen.

"Nothing." She blotted each piece of fish with paper towel, then placed them on a plate and transferred it across to the stove side of the kitchen. "Yep, that James got us all worked up for a few months. Spent some bucks on those mold-testing companies. Some of 'em are just scams, you ask me, dearie." She checked a thermometer stuck to the side of a kettle sitting atop a burner, gas flames dancing along the bottom.

"What happened to James' place? Did he really have

mold?" Hillary halfway hoped the woman was going to invite her to stay for a fish dinner. It would be so nice to have a home like this.

"Not that I know of, but he believed he did." She dipped a filet into her bowl of batter and shook it to drain off excess, then lowered it slowly into the kettle of hot oil. "Became obsessed over it—drove his wife away." A bubbling sound arose, along with a fragrance that made Hillary's stomach growl.

From a door opposite the table she sat at, a burly man burst in, trailed by four children, all howling as to how famished they were. No one paid attention to Hillary. The woman artfully gave each of the five a kiss on the cheek as she continued frying her fish. "Wash up now," she told them in turn. They trooped past Hillary and vanished down a hallway at the other side of the great room.

"Guess that's all you need, dear?" The woman looked at Hillary and turned back to her fish, turning pieces over with wooden spoons.

"Do you know who the people were who James got the mold idea from?" Hillary stood. "The ones in that lowland development?"

"I've got the names somewhere. It was last year or the year before, dearie." The woman rubbed the back of her hand across her damp forehead, brushing back her salt-and-pepper hair. "Can you leave me a card? I can call you tomorrow after the kids get off to school." She smiled apologetically.

"Sure." Hillary got out *The Acorn* business card and

placed it near a wall telephone, next to a calendar full of scribbles, covering each day. "Thank you. I may come back by tomorrow, earlier. I can see myself out. Thanks so much."

She left, wondering if she should make up with Ed. Give marriage a try. Could that be herself ten years from now, married to Ed and the mother of a brood of her own? The matronly woman seemed fulfilled, in a scattered sort of way. Hillary was glad she'd been too upset at the restaurant to take off his grandmother's ring and give it back. Now it hung on a key rack near the front door to her cottage, looking small and lost. The way she felt.

* * *

As Hillary walked out to her car in the soft light of the street lamps, headlights blinded her field of vision. James' garage door lifted and a car pulled into the garage. He got out and opened the rear door, bending into the back seat. Hillary approached and waited until he reappeared with his baby, bundled up in a puffy snowsuit.

"Hello!" She called out quietly, so as not to startle him.

He looked her way, but didn't answer. Instead, he disappeared into his garage, the door closing in noisy jerks.

She decided not to bother the man. She might return the next day and get more information from the motherly woman whose name she did not know. *I don't remember my own mother ever cooking anything for Daddy and me.*

Got to try to reach Violet. Let her know what she's up against from her witch of a mother. Mothers and their sins—commission and omission. What they can do and what they can fail to do. *Which one is worse?*

FIFTEEN

Ed

ED NEEDED to find out the truth. He was desperate to show Hillary his competence. She'd been the one to figure out and capture Melvin the mad butcher last month while duty had called him away to fight the flooding in the Delta.

She'd broken up with him because they didn't know each other well enough she said, and he didn't know about having more kids. He had to convince her he was worth a commitment, worth getting to know over a lifetime. Had to get up his courage to think about children with her. Forty-one. Early forties wasn't all that old to start a family. Was it?

She might have more respect for him if he could solve the mystery of Ted's death—*if* it was a murder. It had been a long five years since his daughter was killed in that Stockton hit-and-run. Death by murder, death by killing. Tricky to uncover all the connections.

It was his day off and he wallowed in a bath of insecurity. Was Hillary doing the right thing to break up with him? He drove to the liquor store near his studio apartment and bought a bottle of Jack Daniels and a five-pack of little cigars. He went home and smoked one, his first cigar in months. He watched reruns of *America's Most Wanted* on TV and sipped Jack Daniels. A show came on about a teenager, a girl killed by a hit and run driver in Detroit. As soon as scenes from her funeral came on, he felt transported to that horrible day they'd buried Mary Beth, the months of hunting for the driver, the year of accusations from Elizabeth. Her disgust with him and that awful week she'd packed up and moved far away, taking loveable little Caron with her.

Funerals. Here was the death of another relationship. Hillary wouldn't even answer his calls. It would be the death of him if he lost her. He knew it.

He switched the channel to basketball and sat on his couch all afternoon. But by the time he made up his mind to drive over to Hillary's cottage, he'd had enough whiskey to know better than to get into the car. Tomorrow, he'd go there. Tomorrow. He had to keep her in his life.

* * *

He and Walt went over the case the next day. At the bottom of the whiteboard, Ed drew a stick figure of Ted in a prone position. "Okay, we have him collapsed and dying. Could it have been cyanide?" He drew a line from Ted's body to the upper left of the whiteboard and printed the word there. "Could it have been sprinkled onto his food or into his drink? Someone at the wake, someone who got close to his table?"

Walt shook his head and cracked his knuckles. "Nah. His symptoms would have been way more obvious."

"Well," Ed drew another line from the body up to the middle of the whiteboard, "could it have been mold spores, a violent reaction to them?" He printed the words and circled them with a question mark next to them. "But how could they act so fast is the question." He frowned at Walt, who shook his head and sat down. "Never heard of such a thing—takes time for the effects to take hold. Got to research something else, maybe some poison that he could have sprayed into the air when he was face to face with Ted?" Walt had lost a few pounds and was looking tired lately, thought Ed. He himself felt plenty tired and depressed himself since Hillary'd backed away. He wasn't thinking clearly.

"Okay, last possibility." He drew a line from the stick figure of the victim to the upper right of the board. "Could have been violent allergic reactions." He printed the words "allergy," "paprika," and "hazelnuts" at the top right of the board.

"I had a horrible reaction years ago after eating a nut

burger followed by hazelnut cake," said Walt, his eyes growing big. "Got covered with welts all over my body."

Ed tried to keep a visual of that sight out of his mind.

"It was on a weekend. Had to get to a doc-in-the-box, get a shot of Benadryl. It's the only kind of cake I won't eat anymore." Walt stood and stretched. "Think I'll make a donut run. Haven't had any for a couple days now." He rubbed his hands together as if warming them up.

"Let's stay with this," Ed said. "Who could have been responsible for each of these items?" He circled all three possible causes of death up on the board. "Problem is, lab reports might not identify which was the biggest factor. Damn labs take way longer than you see 'em on TV. Not sure if we can get a case going here."

Walt picked up a red marker and walked over to the board. Next to the cyanide he printed Blondie, then crossed out both words. Next to spores he printed Mold Man and crossed out those words, and next to allergy he printed Violet.

Ed squinted his eyes. "You've got to be right on Mold Man, the least likely suspect." He took his black marker and added the name of Banker Man beside Blondie's name, and Aunt Helena next to Violet's name. "Blondie and Banker Man have motives, as does Violet. But what in the hell can we do with such a tenuous set of possibilities? Were any of them in it together?"

"Nah," said Walt, pulling his keys out of his pocket. "Too much coordination needed. I can see Blondie and

Banker Man maybe, but not mixed in with Violet, too, although those three did go in and out of the Broome Building a lot, now that I think of it. Got to go pick up something to eat, get over this low blood sugar, be able to think straight. Come on." He walked out toward the parking lot. Ed studied the board for a few seconds more, taking a mental snapshot, help him think things through on the subconscious level.

* * *

What kind of snapshot of him was Hillary carrying around in her head and heart? Should he go over to her place like he vowed to last night? Would she like that or hate it? It was almost better being alone, sitting on his pity pot feeling sorry for himself. Walt might be right about women.

Still, his blood rose just remembering the smell of her the first time he dropped by her cottage, standing in her entry, the spicy scent of her perfume mingled with dried orange peels sitting on the table under the wooden hook she kept her keys on. The truth was, he needed her.

He would keep calling. She'd pick up when she was ready. They both had to want to be together for any chance in hell, to try for heaven here.

SIXTEEN

Violet

ALREADY I FELT MORE COMFORTABLE sitting at Dad's massive desk. Donna was coming by again, to continue planning how to redecorate the office.

I'd had twenty-four hours to let the atmosphere soak in as a space to run the business from. I had an idea of what changes I wanted to make. Hopefully Maggie wouldn't produce some kind of adopted son to challenge me and keep this room with its macho ambience.

When Donna came in, she set down her big tote and twirled in a circle, waving to the four walls. "You'll want all this out of here, right?" She had pulled her blonde hair back into a bun at the nape of her neck.

"Have it moved into storage," I said. "Maybe some-day there will be a family museum." I laughed at the thought.

She looked at me with raised eyebrows. "Remember, Violet—can I call you Violet?"

She used a tone of respect. I nodded. "Yes, that's fine."

"Okay, remember you are the boss. You can either put all this in storage or just outsource it."

"Let's get rid of it," I said. She was good, attuned to my sensibilities. Yes. I wanted these traces of the past gone. Daddy, and Teddy, too. This was *my* company now. *Is my company.*

"Right." She sat down in one of the barrel chairs. "Have you had time to think over the three possibilities I ran by you yesterday?"

"I loved the last one, but I'm not certain yet."

She pulled a sketchpad from her tote. "How do you see yourself as a CEO, where do you want to take Broome Construction?" She got out a stick of charcoal and began doodling circles on the textured page.

I was fascinated. No one had asked me this question before.

Grandad Pat had started us up as a successful statewide company, then Dad had stretched us forward in a hard straight line and built us into a nationwide de-velopment corporation.

"I want to continue in my family's footsteps," I said, "yet take a bit more of a socially responsible tack." *What was I saying?* I felt like I was standing on a diving board that reached out over thin air. And I couldn't see any water below to jump into.

"I want to grow, too." I ran my fingers through my hair, feeling the sticky spray residue. *Grow. Have to stop using aerosols when I get pregnant.*

"Go on . . ." Donna had written down a few words inside her circles: family, social, grow.

"Maybe offer homes at the lower end of the price points?" I sat down in Dad's big chair but immediately stood up. The room felt increasingly oppressive to me, like a silent foe. I knew it was not normal for a CEO to be in question mode. Dad's had been a sure, emphatic voice.

Donna looked up at me. "Keeping safe what has been created, safe for the future? A caretaker owner, would you say?"

God, that sounded lame. "Caretaker?" I felt like squirming when the words came out. "Caretaker. No. Not that." Sounded like someone living in a tiny cottage at the edge of an estate. Someone inconsequential, a loser. Maybe a Lady Chatterley's lover sort. I was in a new world, foreign to me. A world that was a blank slate. I was having to make it up.

Donna kept slowly inscribing circles onto her notepad. She held her short stick of charcoal sideways, making thick lines with soft edges. I felt suddenly inadequate with my accounting background. I needed someone to help me figure out where I wanted to take Broome Construction. Joanna. Fresh from her MBA at Sac State. She knew about running businesses, was a safe sounding board. She would be home soon from her trip to Europe.

"Well," I said, "I'm not sure if it's in your job description, Donna, but go ahead and look at companies run by women." I nodded at her. "Do some research on who's doing what and how. Can you find out what sort of offices they have?" I sat back down in Dad's leather chair. "You can take your time."

Donna was beaming. "Sure. I'll get to work on it soon. Should be fun, really." She stood and pulled the pins out of her hair, loosening the bun and letting her blonde tresses fall in soft waves over her square shoulders. She must feel relaxed around me.

"I look forward to working with you, Violet." She put her sketchpad and charcoal into her tote and reached out to shake my hand. Her grip was warm and firm. I liked her.

* * *

I met Hillary for lunch at the country club. We were seated at a table with a view of the 18th hole. That cute young waiter, Matt, poured lemon water for us and then hovered nearby as Hillary checked over the menu. I decided to go for something different and ordered the Salad Nicoise, while Hillary said she'd have the popular tuna melt.

After Matt left the table, Hillary cleared her throat and picked up a spoon. She thumbed the bowl of the spoon, put it back down, and looked me straight in the eye.

"I interviewed Maggie the other day," she said. I nodded, feeling a familiar heat forming at the sound of my mother's name. *What now?*

"Over at her house. It was to get BC history. Roger wanted to run a piece on the company," she said.

"Sounds good, since I might be planning to take it in a new direction."

"Well, it might be going where no one could have guessed." She shook out her napkin.

"What's that mean?" I nodded as Matt set a basket of bread on the table. I picked up a slice of the club's famous sourdough and dipped it into a saucer of olive oil swimming with balsamic vinegar.

Hillary spread her napkin onto her lap. "Maggie was telling me about wanting to get a son to run BC. Keep to Grandad's vision. Turns out Luisa was listening in while we talked."

"Jesus." I felt a wave of hate rise and set down the bread. Luisa had started working for my parents when I went to college and Maggie lost my free labor.

"Luisa came into the room, head down, and started mumbling. At first, I couldn't understand what she was saying, but then . . ." Hillary looked at me with her lips pursed. She took a slice of bread and began tearing it into small pieces.

The veins in my arms ran cold, as if pumping mercury instead of blood. "Then . . ." I prompted her.

"Luisa confessed she'd had a child," Hillary blurted, "with your father. It was a son. Called him Angel."

"Angel?" I felt paralyzed. "A son?"

"She pronounced it Ahn-hel, you know, the Spanish way. She said your father supported them over the years. Boy's a teenager now, plays high school basketball, Luisa said." Hillary frowned. "I'm sorry to be the messenger, but I wanted you to know . . ." Her voice trailed off.

"What else?" My insides felt turned to stone. High school. Luisa lived in South Stockton, off of Highway 99. I recall hearing that she lived in a community of illegal immigrants.

"Well," Hillary nodded as Matt set our food on the table. "Maggie at first looked horrified but within seconds, she ordered me out of the room and hugged up to Luisa as if they were best friends."

"Jesus," I whispered.

"I think she might be thrilled to learn of this secret love child." Hillary's shoulders slumped and she reached across the table to pat my hand. "I'm so sorry, Vi, but I thought you would want to know."

I shook my head. "That bitch," I hissed.

Hillary scowled so fiercely, I almost had to smile.

I forced myself sit through lunch but could only take a few bites of potato and just poke at the green beans and anchovies.

Hillary did most of the talking, about how she could relate to having a bad mother. Life had been rough after her mother abandoned her father and her and ran off to the South Pacific. I could barely take in a word she said but felt wrapped in her blanket of sympathy and support, with that bitch of a mother of mine.

How could I continue building my vision for BC

with this hanging over me? *Is it true Angel is my father's son?*

   I had to find this devil of a boy.

SEVENTEEN

Violet

I GOT THE BASKETBALL SCHEDULE for Ford High and waited a few days until Buddy was off to a medical conference. The rains had let up and valley tule fog was forming, making for low visibility. My hands laid a film of sweat on the wheel of my Lexus, and I had to be careful not to get into a pileup on the highway. I made it to the high school in Luisa's neighborhood, if she still lived in the same place. I sat in the parking lot, wiping the steering wheel dry with a Kleenex, my head buzzing with fear. I had to see for myself if what Hillary told me was true.

Once inside the overheated gym, I stepped up to the

top bench and sat against the back wall. The score was tied at 25. The home crowd cheered as a tall teen smashed the ball through the basket in a vicious dunk, so fast my eyes missed it. I stared at the young man who'd made the play, now racing back down the court to the other end.

It must be him. No one else on either team had that bright orange hair standing helter-skelter. He looked so much like Grandad.

The loud squeaks of players' shoes rattled my thoughts. In the distance, church bells sounded evening devotions. How could my father, my Catholic father, sire a love child and keep it a secret all these years?

The stench of sweaty bodies overcame me. I closed my eyes. The horn blew for halftime. I watched the players crowd around their coach. The tall redheaded boy turned and stared straight at me for a second. His face was sprinkled with freckles, just like Grandad Pat's.

I left the gym. What was I going to do about this teenaged boy? How old was he? Could I chance his being a legitimate blood relative? I felt lost and didn't know where to turn.

As I drove home along Highway 99, I passed a lighted billboard advertising psychic readings by Madame Zoltar. In small print were words that caught my eyes in the split second it took to speed by: Inquire about love spells.

Love spells? What other kinds of spells were there? My heart raced. I slowed down, took the next off ramp and circled back along the frontage road. This time, I drove slowly past the billboard and rechecked the phone number for Madame Zoltar. Would I have the guts to call her? My palms slid on the steering wheel and I had to rub my hands on my pants to safely continue down the highway.

This was getting too weird. Who was it that Joanna had consulted about starting up her restaurant business? When she told me, I thought she was on the edge of crazy, with her MBA and all. Why would she need that extra assurance. But now everything clicked.

I pulled off the freeway, parked at a well-lit gas station and lifted my new cell phone off its dashboard holder. I flipped it open and hit speed dial for Joanna, praying she was home from her trip.

She picked up the phone. "Hey, Cuz." I wasn't in the mood to waste words. "Remember that psychic you said you talked to before going ahead with your restaurant plans?"

"Sure, but you're sitting pretty at BC now, yes?"

I couldn't let her know how much turmoil I was in. "I need help on how to fit into the 'old boys club' better. You know?" It wasn't a lie.

"Yeah. Running alongside the good-ol'-boys will keep us fit, all right." Joanna laughed. "Okay, her name is weird. Hecaterine, but she has everyone call her Caty. I've known her for years. She volunteers at the library in town. She gave me the green light for my restaurant, like I told you. So far, I trust her."

"Got her number handy?" I poked around in the console for a notebook and pen.

"Most days, she's over at that new shop in Clearwater. It's a colorful little place if you're not allergic to incense. Candles, Crystals, and Cards. I felt at home there—they had my favorite yoga music playing—Shri Ram." She started chanting in low tones.

Once Joanna got going, she was hard to stop.

"I've had this sixth sense all day that I need to see her," I interrupted. Joanna was a believer in going with your intuition. "Is she available in the evenings?"

"She sees clients at home, too. By referral only, so tell her I gave you her name. I paid her a fat retainer, so ask her to put it on my bill."

"Ready for the number. Shoot." I felt like shooting something myself.

"Her full name is Hecaterine Crowley. Old Dr. Crowley was her dad. Remember him?" Joanna was off topic again.

"I'm in kind of a hurry, Jojo." I tried to keep my voice calm.

"Sorry. Here's her number, home first, then the shop." She got through the two numbers without veering into another subject.

"Thanks, Cuz. I owe you."

"I'm just making up for your help with the restaurant planning. The only thing we might put a question mark by is that Czech goulash." She sighed.

"We don't know if that was the issue with Ted," I said. I could feel my stomach twist into a tight knot.

After we hung up, I sat for several minutes and

rubbed my belly in small circles, taking deep breaths until I got past the guilt that popped up each time I thought about Ted.

Joanna's psychic would be much better than going to the unknown Madame Zoltar. I punched in Caty's home number.

I would see her as soon as I could about this Angel problem—and do whatever she told me. I drove home through the fog.

EIGHTEEN

Hillary

HILLARY HEADED TO THE COLLEGE to check on her students. She hoped she hadn't caused Violet too much suffering, but a love child shouldn't be kept a secret. Motherhood. What a messy business, married or not. Still, she couldn't ignore the hole in her heart but Ed didn't know if he wanted more children. Was she ever going to have a family of her own?

Daniel was the only student in the newsroom, the pressure of a deadline not yet building. She read through his story. Clearwater College's interior design program had won runner-up in a national competition. The program was lucky to have BC's Donna Lister on their advisory board. Hillary gave Daniel a couple tips on polishing the story and then drove over to *The Acorn*.

Not only had Mildred brought in homemade brownies, but Roger was back from San Francisco.

"Hey, Dopey!" Roger grinned from his desk. He looked more relaxed than she'd ever seen him.

"The trip did you good." She smiled at her editor and got herself the biggest brownie from the pan. The hell with the diet.

"I hear I missed some big doings in town last weekend." He turned serious. "That family of yours caused mega drama over at Holy Family, girl." He stood and gave Hillary a hug. "I'm sorry about your cousin Ted."

It was comforting to have a boss who was a friend, maybe her only friend. But she couldn't picture asking him to be her maid of honor. And Violet sure wasn't going to feel close to her now since that bad news she'd delivered. She had no other friends or family she could have asked.

"That's not the worst part." She rolled her chair over next to Roger's. "Ted's cause of death is not known yet."

"What?" He stared at her, his eyebrows raised high.

"It seemed like he was choking on his food, or having an epileptic fit, really, when it was happening. He fell to the floor at the reception after the funeral. Right in the church hall."

Mildred was staring at the two of them. Hillary realized she was shouting and lowered her voice. "Yes, he was at a head table with some men from the bank sitting nearby. Ted cut one of them off when he was giving a eulogy. Wonder what their relationship was."

Roger nodded. "I heard there were demonstrators at the service?"

"Just one. A man with a sign about mold in BC houses, chanting about babies dying." Hillary shook her head. "I took that student Natalie out to a Broome development to try and find the guy, but no luck so far." Hillary described her visit to the homeowner she had started to think of as another Mold Man. He wasn't the frenzied guy who'd run around in the parish hall, though.

"So it could be a homicide? That's what you're saying?" Roger sat up straighter. "Bankers? Disgruntled buyers?"

"Detectives are looking at BC's interior designer, too, a woman named Donna Lister, and even wondering about Violet, Ted's sister."

"And what's your source on that?" Roger grinned and tugged at his caramel-colored vest. "Still cozy with Mr. Fiancé?"

Hillary couldn't help but blush. Roger had been there Thanksgiving Day when Ed proposed and gave her his grandmother's diamond.

"That's over now," she said, and took a big bite out of her brownie, praying Roger would let it drop. "But I think they are way off-base suspecting those women." She thought Ed was off-base about several other things, too, but kept that to herself.

"It's over? You're free again?" He stood and gave her a high five. "Let the good times roll!"

How humiliating to have to admit another failed relationship. Roger already thought straight couples were too wrapped up in their ideas of wedded bliss.

Hillary finished her brownie and asked Mildred for the recipe. Then she checked her email and was relieved to find nothing new from Charles. She Googled around on the subject of mortgage bankers. Seemed that many loans were now being bundled into derivatives, offering substantial returns on investments.

Without the list of names from the funeral, Hillary couldn't identify the banker Ted cut off at the reception. Ed would have that list. She sighed.

But still, she needed to get background information, talk to a mortgage lender. She sensed that people were buying these new homes who couldn't really afford them. Look at that man yesterday with the baby, another Mold Man. He was all alone, didn't even appear to be holding a job. How could he afford that big house he was rattling around in with his sick baby?

Hillary had covered real estate for a few years when she was with *The Sacramento Bee*. That was back at the start of the housing boom. The market was so hot now, people were almost under a spell, lining up to buy houses in new developments as if there was going to be some kind of shortage. She'd read about couples who camped out in developments up in Elk Grove, to be first in line for a drawing to see who would get to buy the houses in a new release.

* * *

Hillary drove through the tule fog over to the Nor-Cal Mortgage office on Main Street. It was in a Tuscan-style building, similar to many of the homes in the development she'd driven through with Natalie. She was beginning to rethink her earlier attraction to this style.

She entered the NorCal foyer and walked up to a striking young woman, slim to the point of skeletal. The woman smiled brightly at Hillary. "How may we serve you?" she asked.

"I'd like to talk to one of your loan brokers, for a story." Hillary flashed her press card.

"They are all busy with clients right now, but I can make an appointment for you." The woman hit a few keys on her computer keyboard. "Would you care to say what the story's about?"

Hillary described her interest in the burgeoning housing market in San Joaquin Valley, especially connected to the Broome Construction developments.

"Mr. Perignon should be a good one for you to talk to. He'll be available at four this afternoon. Would you like to come in then?"

Hillary nodded and gave one of her business cards to the woman, who typed slowly into the computer, hit the enter key and nodded. "Okay, you're all set."

Driving back to the college newsroom, Hillary hoped more students had come in. They were almost like a family to her. Got to keep busy, block out thoughts of Ed and any kind of happily-ever-after life.

* * *

The email from Charles was plenty of diversion. Before, he'd sent to the *Acorn* office, but now he'd found her college email address. She couldn't let the students see this. The Subject line read: "Plagiarism Probe Set." He'd forwarded a story about another professor under suspicion—this time at Harvard—for using "others" work without attribution in papers he published in academic journals.

Damn that Charles. He never added any of his own comments. Just wanted to torment her. Probably wanted to just yank her chain. Chain. She was chained to Charles by her guilt over those two times she'd panicked at Colombia. Stories about mothers. Bad mothers. That was her downfall. It would be a challenge to write about BC when Maggie was such a horrible creature with her own daughter, Violet.

Hillary had to get onto a different tack, get moving on a story about the hot housing market, the financial side. Four o'clock couldn't come soon enough.

* * *

The muscular middle-aged man grinned and ran his fingers through his silver-shot black hair. "Perignon. Yes. The same as that fancy champagne. Here." He touched the back of a burgundy leather chair for Hillary to take a seat.

"What can I do for you? Broome, is it? In the construction company family?"

She explained her loose connection to BC and went

on to ask him about the way mortgages were now being approved. "Seems like more people are getting loans now than I would have thought could qualify, at least in the past."

"Well, regulations have been relaxed to allow for equity in achieving the American Dream of home ownership. Yes, indeed." He picked up a set of legal-sized folders from the right side of his desk. "And . . ." He held up the folders with both hands and waved them in the air. "And, at the same time, offering opportunities for others to buy into bundled loans as equity investments. It's a win-win."

He set the folders on his desk, beaming at them as if he were reviewing a parade of models in a new automobile line. "You in the market, young lady?"

Flustered, Hillary flashed on the model homes she'd pictured as a place for Ed and her. That was over now. She ignored the question. "Do you happen to know who handles the loans for Broome Construction? I was trying to contact a man I think was at Robert Broome's funeral, so I could talk to him as well." She worried there would be some kind of hush-hush around identifying specific mortgage bankers.

"Well, it was probably Jake Mortenson. We would love to get BC's business away from him, that's for sure. But he's connected with big players and not just in America. Here at NorCal we have to take what crumbs we can find on the table." He tapped the surfaced of the manila folders and stood as if to end the conversation. "Still, what blesses one, blesses all, as my mother used to say."

Hillary thanked him for his time and drove over to *The Acorn*. Dollars and cents—that's what she needed to focus on—forget about marriages, mother and daughter messy bits. Follow the money. Was there some reason Mortenson might have wanted Ted out of the way?

NINETEEN

Violet

WHEN I TRIED CATY'S HOME NUMBER, I was lucky enough to have her answer. After I identified myself, Caty said she remembered Joanna and even recalled her mentioning a cousin named Violet who might go into business with her. She suggested I come to her house the next evening. It was more private than the candle shop, she said, and gave me her address, in the old part of Lodi.

* * *

I drove down Caty's quiet street, lined with modest

crackerbox houses, nothing to suggest anything other-worldly. Her porch light was shaped like a candle, and a low Ommmm tone reverberated after I pushed her door-bell. Amazed to find myself consulting a psychic, I shivered in the cold and wondered if Caty's conservative neighbors knew how she made her living.

The door opened to a short, plump woman in her fifties. She wore a yellow caftan and had long black hair piled up in a topknot. The smell of incense wafted out the door, and I could hear some kind of East Indian music from inside.

"Welcome, Violet!" she cried, waving me through the front door, past a carved wooden screen, and into a toasty living room. "Call me Caty. Please come in and make yourself at home. I feel connected to you already through your cousin Joanna."

She nodded in the direction of a round oak table at the side of the room. I put my purse on her rose-colored carpet and dropped into a comfortable wing chair. Caty sat down opposite me. There was no crystal ball or Tarot cards on the table, I noticed. Nothing there except a square box of tissues and a small bowl of uncooked white rice. Beyond the table was a tall bookshelf, dividing this room from some other. The bookshelf was crammed, holding things of all sorts, books huge and small, a few old enough to have peeling covers and others that looked like comic books. Some shelves held candles and other objects, most of which I could not identify. One tattered book had a title that seemed to glow and reach out to me: *Poisonous Plants, the Deadly Deception*. I blinked several times and turned toward Caty. Her slight smile and warm brown eyes invited secrets.

"I've never done this before," I blurted. "But I've got a huge problem I just learned about." Suddenly, my arms felt drained of blood, like I might pass out, opening up like this to a stranger.

"Not to worry, Vi," Caty said. "May I call you Vi?"

Only my mother ever had called me that. And then I hated it. The way she said it made it sound like "vile." But coming from Caty, the name sounded like it was perfect for me. *Vi*. I nodded.

"Many people come to me," she went on, "new to the practice of reaching out beyond the visible. It's not all that mysterious, just not commonly done."

I nodded, my limbs warming back up. Her voice was tranquilizing.

"All it does is let you take a look at your life and the path you are on. If there is some way I can assist, I offer suggestions to that end as well. Do you have questions before I start?"

"How come you can help people in this way?" I needed assurance this was not black magic out of thin air, that she had traveled some legitimate path to her practice. I was caught between feeling skeptical of working with a psychic, yet desperate for help in the threat of Angel.

"I don't generally talk about myself but since you clearly need to know, my intuitive ability is a gift from my mother. She was a scholar, who studied the age of the goddess. She helped Marija Gimbutas at archeological digs. Perhaps you've heard of her?" Caty stood and took a couple thick books off her shelf and set them on the table.

She handed over one of the volumes. "This describes some of their work." The book was titled *The Language of the Goddess*. "My mother assisted in selecting dig sites in Europe in the eighties. She helped unearth artifacts that demonstrate the central role of the feminine in the Neolithic period."

I leafed through the book, awed by the images of females in all sorts of shapes, sizes, and situations. It hit me that if only this kind of culture had survived, I would not have to fight for my place in the company.

"Then on my father's side," Caty murmured as I studied the book open on the table, "he was different, too. A doctor who still went on house calls until the day he died. I inherited his black medical bag, still loaded with instruments for healing." She smiled. "I learned a lot, too, from volunteer work with public librarians in Lodi—those women know far more than how to check out a book."

My hope soared. *Was finding Caty preordained to make up for all those years with Maggie against me?* Now to tell her what I needed and wanted. Or sit still, wait to see if she could intuit it on her own.

Caty put the books back on the shelf. She set them right next to that book with the glowing cover. I itched to hold it.

After she lifted two or three different candles off the shelf and put them back down, Caty selected a short thick white one and set it onto the raw rice in the bowl, rotating it gently as if to ensconce it. She flicked on a butane lighter wand, lit the candle, and watched it for a long minute before she spoke.

"You face a set of dreadful decisions—and soon. You will be able to make them because of your core strength." She lifted her head and gazed at me, expressionless. "But they may cost you your life."

Her words yanked at my heart and left me speechless. *My life. Angel's life.*

"But," I found my voice. "I don't need anyone's life. I just need to have a person, a young man, removed from here, maybe move away, say to a place like Mexico?" I was pretty sure Luisa was an illegal immigrant, and if I turned her in, she might have to leave the U.S. Surely her Angel son would go with her, wouldn't he?

"It's more to protect myself," I went on, "from my mother. She wants to push me out of our family business, bring in a male to take my place." Tears were rolling down my cheeks but I didn't bother wiping them. Was I going to fall over the edge?

Caty was instantly attuned to my desire. "I will give you a spell of protection. This should not harm others if you do it right, but only keep your enemies powerless."

I sat there, tears flowing as I took in her every word.

"You need to get some dirt, about a cupful, from your mother's house. Can you do that?" She raised her dark eyebrows at me.

Dirt? I nodded, and reached around the short candle for a tissue.

"You then take that dirt and sprinkle it in all four corners of your workplace. It helps if you can get a silent witness, too."

I waited but she sat back in her chair, and closed her eyes. Not wanting to break in, I let several minutes pass before I spoke. "Is that all?" It sounded too easy.

Caty's eyes remained shut. "It sounds simple but it's not. The dirt is part of the earth and has stability and power. It has absorbed the energies of your enemy who has walked it over the years." She sat motionless, eyes still closed. "And it has knowledge of you, deep unspoken knowledge, and will absorb knowledge of where you carry and sprinkle it. It will use the energy of your enemy to shield you from her."

We sat together for another few minutes, not speaking. It was hard to believe something so simple might work to protect me from Maggie and her Angel. I felt I needed more. That book. It was still glowing, almost flashing, like it was on fire inside. Caty must have felt the invisible heat from the book. She opened her eyes. "You may borrow any of my books if you want to use them on your own. I cannot be responsible for your work."

Caty rose and smoothed the front of her yellow caftan down across her ample belly. "Let me know how this turns out, if you wish, Vi." She nodded. "Or not. Sometimes it's better for me to be kept in the dark." She shook her head slowly. "Go now."

It felt so formal. I had been dismissed. The book's title had faded into a series of letters not unlike those running down the spines of its fellows. But it felt branded into my mind.

Now Caty's bizarre directions were sounding almost reasonable. I had to follow them.

I left and drove straight to Maggie's house. There was no moon but I could see the gate. It was locked but the dirt next to the flagstones looked easy to get to. I would go home and get a spoon and a cup. It had to be tonight. This was the last night of Buddy's medical conference. And I could sprinkle the dirt easily tomorrow.

I'd have to put off redecorating Dad's office. This might just do the trick.

Disable his Angel.

TWENTY

Hillary

THE VIRGIN MARY stood in a candle-lit side chapel, her blue veil topped with a plumeria lei that fell to her feet, standing on a globe of the earth. Hillary leaned forward to smell the creamy flowers when suddenly Mary's gown morphed into a grass skirt and her hips swayed in a slow hula dance. Hillary's shoulders moved to the same rhythm. She breathed slowly and her body filled with peace. The virgin's face dimmed until her features faded to a black and white photo of Hillary's young mother—laughing with joy looking up at Hillary's father, who was holding her as a newborn. Hillary could sense herself waking up and struggled to stay asleep, but it was no use.

She lay in bed, eyes closed, reliving the dream. *If only*. At least she had lunch with Sarah to look forward to.

* * *

On the noontime drive to Little Joe's, Anne Murray's song about a lover who needed her came blasting into Hillary's car, hitting her in the heart. *You needed me*. It was a kind of prison to need anyone. Or be needed. It was. Hillary switched to the public radio station for the news. The modulated voice was describing 2005 as the Year of Cork City, Ireland, the European Capital of Culture. *Ireland. Where Grandad Patrick was from*. What a relief to listen to facts. Music let in too much pain.

* * *

She strode in with energy, admiring the restaurant's colorful wall. Little Joe kept it covered year round with lacy placemats featuring tiny skulls and Spanish words cut into tissue paper. It reminded her of cutting out strings of snowflakes and paper dolls with joined hands when she was in kindergarten. Before she learned that *happily ever after* was just in fairy tales.

Sarah was seated in what had become their booth. Hillary hoped the Day of the Dead wall didn't forecast the death of the little café. At times, she and Sarah were the only customers, but today it was nearly half full. Maybe the students' articles spotlighting local entrepreneurs were making a difference.

Hillary bent down and gave the older woman a gentle hug.

Sarah grinned and gestured toward the seat opposite, her arms still mottled with bruises from the ordeal Hillary rescued her from last month. Melvin the mad butcher had almost added Sarah to his crazy efforts to stop superstores from putting little businesses to death. Hillary was still amazed at her own heroic strength in saving Sarah. Amazed and proud, too.

"Joe's bringing our usual," Sarah said.

Our usual. Sweet. Maybe this is what it's like to have a mother.

Hillary slid into her side of the burgundy leatherette booth, well worn over the years, comfortable to sit and chat in. If she'd been asked, Hillary might have compared it to a nest where she somehow felt cared for.

Sarah pulled a napkin from the chrome box on the table. "Now that Melvin is in jail, waiting for his trial," she said, folding the napkin into paper triangles, "his house and mine are the only two on our street unsold and standing in the way of development. Broome Construction wants to call it Heavenly Acres. Supposed to be like a Sun City. It's for what they call active adults, but it's really for us old folks who can still get around."

Sarah brushed back her bangs, as white as the paper napkin she fiddled with. "I'm getting a lot of pressure to sell. I know you're related, honey, but they seem like greedy giants, not so different from those superstores that got poor Melvin into a deranged state."

Little Joe came to their table, plates of grilled cheese

sandwiches on one arm, a big salad bowl in the other. After setting the sandwiches down, he tossed grapes and mandarins together with fresh greens and toasted walnuts from the orchards of Morada. "Enjoy your 'Local Jump-up,'" he said, referring to the salad's name.

Hillary loved the man's showmanship. She thanked him and turned back to Sarah. "Where would you live if you sold?"

She would hate to see Sarah move back East to live with her grown children. Hillary picked up her sandwich, careful to keep the melted cheese from stringing across her lap, and raised her eyebrows at the motherly woman.

"That's the thing," Sarah said. "I hate getting in the way of progress, as they call it, but I can't afford to live in one of the new places they're building either."

Hillary's cell rang and she glanced at the caller ID.

Ed again. She was determined to ignore him. She turned off the ringer, and put her phone in her pants pocket, hoping Sarah hadn't seen the caller ID. Even worse would be if Sarah noticed the absence of the diamond ring. Hillary didn't feel like discussing her poor judgment in thinking it was a good idea to run off and marry a man she barely knew.

But Sarah had heard and seen. "How's Ed doing this week, honey?"

Hillary flushed. She hated that tendency, which fit with her redheaded complexion. There hadn't been anything recently to bring roses to her cheeks, though, until she met Ed a couple months ago in the superstore mayhem. Now, instead of blushing with joy, she was hot with embarrassment.

Sarah took a bite of gleaming leafy greens and chewed vigorously before she spoke again. "Wouldn't bother me if you took his call. I like that young man. What's more, he needs you. I hope you know that."

Nervous, Hillary cut the already tiny mandarin segment in two and wondered if she should admit to Sarah that she had nobody to ask to stand up with her. There was Roger, of course, but he was so riled up about gays not being allowed to marry, she felt certain he would not want to be a wedding attendant. Cousins Joanna and Violet were busy with their own lives and she'd never been all that close to them anyway. Her father was six feet under now, and her mother—well, who knew where she was. The lawyers had been sending her BC checks all these years. She had to ask them where they were mailed to. *Do I really want to know?*

Hillary cut up as many large salad pieces as she could find, feeling overcome with reserve. Rain beat against the café windows. It was like that stormy day last month when she'd had to gather her courage and go rescue Sarah.

Hillary took a deep breath and sighed. "Sarah?"

"Yes, honey?" Sarah set down her salad fork.

"How long did you know John before you married?" Hillary's stomach tightened.

"Why we up and ran off to Reno three weeks after he walked in the door of the Rancheria store. Didn't I ever tell you about that?" Sarah's eyes glistened.

"Believe it or not, Melvin's mother and I were best friends back then in Shingle Springs. She would come and stay over, sometimes for weeks. Think she liked me better than I liked her, though. Or in a different way. It was kind of a sad case. She came down to Lodi and found Melvin's father running the butcher shop in John's store. Married him so's she could be near me."

Sarah's face had a dreamy faraway look to it. "We were more like soul sisters. Nothing physical." Hillary didn't know what to say.

"Yes, honey!" Sarah snapped back to the present and she laughed. "We four did everything together all those years. Those two marriages were as strong as they come.

"And you all had children, didn't you?"

"My, yes, but we had to do some finagling to get the men to agree. They were so wrapped up in Stoney's Market, I'm afraid they didn't pay good attention to the kids." She sighed.

"Now all of those darlings are gone—some for good, some far away, poor Melvin in prison. Feel like I'm some kind of old lady orphan." Sarah frowned and looked away. "Know what I mean?"

Hillary wanted to get up and sit beside Sarah, put her arm around her in comfort, but she sat frozen to the leatherette bench. She played with the crust of her sandwich, still golden though the cheese was cold and firm.

"I do." Hillary propped her elbows on the table and rubbed her eyes. "I know because that's how I feel since my father died. It hasn't even been a year and it's horrible, isn't it?"

Sarah turned back to Hillary. "It's just hard, that's all. But you can't go around it. You have to go through it." She nodded. "It was a blessing, what John and I had all those years. A blessing I would not trade for anything."

Hillary nodded.

"I have a feeling Ed is that kind of man, honey." Sarah reached across the table to pat Hillary's hand. "You can't make a dream come true by running away from it, you know."

Hillary swallowed. The inside of her chest felt like it was on fire. An impulse to make up with Ed, feel his arms around her, overpowered her. She could work on Ed, get him to want kids with her. And, maybe Sarah would stand up with her in Reno.

Suddenly, Hillary felt ashamed of herself. Sarah wouldn't want to be a witness at a wedding when she had lost her husband just a little over a month ago.

Sarah lifted her water glass. "Here's to happiness and going for it!"

Hillary wished she had a mother like Sarah. She had a sudden flash of Sarah settled in with her and Ed in some idyllic future.

"Sarah," Hillary said. She felt overtaken with hope and let go of the sandwich crusts. She dusted her hands off. "Well, I was wondering if you are free in the next few days? Free for a trip to Reno?"

"No need to check my social calendar. It's barely got anything on it. If you're asking me to stand in for mother of the bride, hell yes!" She laughed and reached across the table to take Hillary's hands in hers and give them a squeeze. "Get your courage up, girl."

Hillary blushed. Her cell phone vibrated against her leg. She eyed Sarah and answered Ed's call.

TWENTY-ONE

Violet

I WAS AMAZED. It had been so easy. Maggie had no dogs and the others on Lincoln Road were too far away to set off a warning. I took along my latest collector's doll as a witness, finally getting some good out of one of those presents for girls only. I stood her up against the white picket gate, her blue eyes staring straight ahead, her blonde curls perfect as ever, her mouth shut. My silent witness.

The soil was packed flat near the flagstone walk but rains had left it soft. I filled a cupful with no problem. I took it home and spread it out on a newspaper in the garage to dry out.

This morning I poked the dirt around to make it nice and crumbly. I filled up an empty jelly jar with it and took a few leftover spoonfuls out to sprinkle by my front door. Just in case.

I stuck the jelly jar into a tote bag. Didn't give me the sleek professional look I was going after, but Kaylyn wouldn't notice that. I walked in and told her I didn't want to be disturbed, had to focus on a new project.

Now I was grateful for Dad's dark brown carpet. I'd have to somehow keep this carpet in Donna's redo plans. I got the glass jar out and set it on his desk. *My desk.* Should have brought a spoon, but sprinkling from the jar was maybe even better.

Sprinkle, Caty had said. Sprinkle the dirt in all four corners of your workspace. It will protect you from harm.

Dazed, I unscrewed the lid slowly, and set the jar on the desk blotter. I'd never tried anything like this before. I held it with both hands, tight. It had to work.

The buzz of the intercom made me jump. A little dirt fell out onto the desk blotter.

"I told you I didn't want to be disturbed," I hissed into the receiver.

"It's a woman, your cousin Hillary. Says it's important." Kaylyn's voice was crisp as ever.

"Jesus, woman." *She couldn't respect my orders, even such a modest one?* "Tell her I'll call her back later." I slammed the phone down and used a couple of my new business cards to scrape up the spilled soil and put it back into the jar.

I needed all the protection I could get. The soft dark

soil dropped into the southeast corner of the office with ease. I stepped back, tapped it a couple times with my toe. Could hardly make it out from the dense pile of dark brown wool carpet. I smiled and sprinkled the other three corners.

* * *

I sat at Dad's desk, my desk, for a long minute, absorbing the new energy in the room.

After I felt back to normal, I returned Hillary's call. She was all excited. Chattered on so fast I could barely make out what she was talking about. Big deal. She was running off to Reno, getting married to that detective.

Him.

I needed to stay on his good side. Get him past suspecting me of harming Teddy. Which I never had anything to do with anyway. Wishing is not a crime.

Neither is protecting yourself.

I told Hillary I was happy for them and said it might be fun to have a party after they got back. The family needed something to celebrate. We could hold it at the new BC clubhouse, over off I-5, I said.

Without warning, she changed the subject. "So, what have you done about Angel?"

I was shocked that she might guess what I was up to.

"I'm worried that Maggie might use him against you," Hillary said.

"I've got to try to talk to her," I sputtered, "talk some sense into her." That would be the day.

Hillary said she'd phone me when they got back from Reno. I told her I'd start in planning a little reception over at the clubhouse.

But I had in mind something splashy. It would be a good way to show everyone how well I could manage things.

TWENTY-TWO

Hillary

HILLARY SEARCHED through her closet, pulling each coat hanger forward in turn. Ed didn't love her for her clothes, she reminded herself, looking at the navy blazer and matching pants she'd had on the day she met him. It had only been a couple months but they'd been through a lot. Well not a lot, but going through breaking up and then getting to the other side. That was something. It felt like a lot. Her antique diamond sparkled even in the dim light of the small cottage closet. She was proud of herself, pushing through her own insecurity, convincing Ed she would be there for the long haul.

She had slid the ring back on her finger and broken

the speed limit driving over to his studio apartment. Walked right in, waved her ring finger in front of his eyes, and sat right down. Told him the story of her mother and father, what she'd learned from her father about commitment. That she could see in Ed that kind of caring. They talked for hours.

They'd even discussed the ring issue and if he wanted a wedding band. "I thought of getting you a jade ring to match your eyes," she said.

"No worries. I'm yours, ring or no ring." Ed nuzzled her cheek. "A ring didn't do any good in the past. Better to have a ring around my heart, like you do."

"You are so romantic," she said. Their words morphed into kisses. And more kisses.

The elopement was on again. This time with more fervor.

She'd never visualized herself in a fancy wedding gown, as some girls did. Her artist mother had made fun of brides decked out in traditional garb and called them unimaginative. As a child, Hillary was dressed in bright print fabrics her mother created and made into her own children's clothing line.

Years later Hillary understood these accomplishments were part of her mother's search for a kind of fame to match her husband's standing as a journalist. Her mother made no secret of her envy of his position as a newsman for the Sacramento bureau of the Los Angeles Chronicle.

At each of his front-page bylines, her mother would pound herself in the chest with a fist. "Feels like a knife to the heart," she'd say. Hillary could still see it in her mind's eye, still feel the torn sensations.

Soon after her mother ran off to the South Pacific with her art teacher, Hillary had taken to wearing plain colors, solids in earthy shades, tones her father advised when he took her shopping. She grew to feel at home in muted colors that he said set off her coppery hair and fair skin—shades of green, brown, and gold.

Now Hillary lifted a wool suit jacket off the rod. Nipped in at the waist and cut in a curvy style to complement her plus size, the coffee-colored outfit would be perfect for this December weather.

Among her blouses she found a long-sleeved silk shirt in a rich gold tone.

She rummaged through her top drawer and pulled out a gauzy scarf in emerald green, turquoise, and gold. It would be easy to drape over her head like a veil. Her new knee-high boots in dark chocolate brown would finish off the casual look. She smiled at the vision of herself, dressed in a sort of un-wedding ensemble.

* * *

After she finished packing for the two nights away, she checked the furnace, turning it down to 52 degrees, and locked up the cottage. By five, she was on the road to Sarah's in Lodi, where Ed and Walt would meet up with them to caravan to Reno. Ed didn't want to drive his sheriff's unmarked, so the plan was for Walt to drive his Oldsmobile and Hillary to follow in her VW Golf.

Sarah was all ready to go. "I'm thrilled you asked me," she said. "My kids don't seem like they're ever going to get married, just work forever out in New York." She wrinkled her nose. "The Big Apple."

Hillary gave her a hug. "I like it here in the big valley even better," she said. "The weather for our trip is supposed to be good. Clear with a half moon, so some light for our journey."

The two men arrived just then, and Hillary loved the goofy grin plastered on Ed's face. "All set for our adventure?" He hugged Hillary with gusto, and then Sarah, too. "We'll go first and keep you in Walt's rearview. He'll bring you home tomorrow, Sarah, after the big event." He waggled his eyebrows and made Hillary's heart swell with happiness. *This man is the right one. Yes.*

They piled into the two cars and headed north on Highway 99 to Sacramento, then merged onto I-80 east and on toward the Sierra Nevada Mountains.

By the time they reached Auburn, scattered rain had started falling. Hillary handed her cell phone to Sarah. "Give Ed a call. Make sure they know what our headlight pattern looks like. This rain was not in the forecast." She turned on the local news to listen for weather updates.

Sarah sat staring at the phone. Hillary reached over and took it back. She hadn't realized that Sarah didn't know how to operate a cell phone. She glanced down to hit Ed's speed-dial number, looking up in time to veer away from the cliff edge of the highway as it curved around a sharp turn. She handed the phone back to Sarah. "It's ringing, yes?"

They should have practiced this before they set out. The rain was coming faster now. Hillary turned down the radio volume, grateful for the steering wheel control buttons.

"Hi Ed. Hillary wants to be sure you can tell our lights." Sarah must have gotten through to his phone. "Don't lose us in your rearview. She's worried about the rain and listening to the weather reports."

Hillary could hear Ed's deep voice coming through the phone but she couldn't make out his words. He sounded reassuring, though. That voice—it was a comfort like Daddy's. When he was alive. A sadness washed over her and she felt her chest constrict.

"We're right behind you. Tell Walt not to make any sudden stops." Sarah said good-bye.

Hillary glanced at Sarah, who sat staring at the phone. "Just hit the End button. That will hang up the call."

She turned the radio back up just in time to hear of an unpredicted winter storm headed down from Alaska. Snow was expected at 4,000 feet and motorists were advised to carry chains.

Chains. Hillary had not considered that possibility. "Call Ed back. See what he thinks. Where would we get chains?" She could feel the Golf's tires gripping the wet road surface.

Evidently, Sarah had figured out how to use the phone. Hillary could hear Ed's voice booming over the line, but Sarah was offering just a few umms and ahs before she said goodbye. "Ed has the Highway Patrol roadside station turned on," she said. "The storm warning is a standard precaution. We should be able to beat it, get over Donner Summit and down before chains are needed. But that means we have to push on without stopping."

Hillary exhaled, realizing she'd been holding her breath. They drove by the lights of Sugar Bowl Ski Resort. "Great. We can't even stop for a bathroom break. I need to pee."

"For your sake, I won't tell any jokes," Sarah said, making Hillary laugh. It was going to be a long hour getting across Donner Pass. Rain fell steadily as they ascended into the Sierra Nevadas. Grateful the traffic was not super light, Hillary was relieved they would not be isolated in case of car trouble. The auto association could not be expected to come to their rescue up here.

Her Volkswagen Golf was small but powerful and she had made it a habit to keep it well maintained. She wondered about Walt's Oldsmobile, though.

They drove through the dark. Hillary felt more comfortable driving the mountain highway at night than in daylight. This way she couldn't see the cliff edges, since the cloud cover kept out moonlight. The rain turned to sleet with visibility maybe twenty feet. The Golf's temperature display showed it had fallen to thirty-three degrees outside. The radio kept announcing a forecast for snow. Hillary barely made out the sign for Donner Summit. Over seven-thousand feet with a steep downgrade to come.

They began their descent.

The strain of watching the road through sleety drizzle and having to keep a safe distance from Walt's car and Highway 80's cliff edges kept Hillary and Sarah boxed into a tense silence. Hillary was startled when Walt's right turn signal came on and he pulled over into a vista point turnout. Hillary braked the Golf, reassured once more when the brakes held without swerving. She turned in behind Walt's car, worried but hoping for a bathroom.

"What's wrong?" she yelled as she got out. The vista point showcased a black nightscape. The two men were already standing by the wide open doors of Walt's car.

"Walt wants to check the tires. Felt some swerving." Ed reached into the back seat of the two-door sedan to pull out a parka with a fur-trimmed hood. "How you doing?"

"I need a bathroom." Hillary walked up close to Ed. She kissed him and rubbed noses with him. "Mr. Eddy Eskimo." He laughed and hugged her tight. "Let me go," she said. "I've got to go find some privacy."

Ed walked over to Walt, circling his car and checking out each tire with a flashlight.

Hillary crossed the parking lot and spotted a trash bin she could use as a shield, grateful for that little privacy and the Kleenex in her pocket.

As she walked back to the cars, she couldn't hear the rain anymore. Stretching out her hands, palms up, she watched with delight and terror as snowflakes dropped silently into her palm. She rejoined the men, standing at the open doors of Walt's car. "It's snowing, guys. We'll have a white wedding." The three of them laughed.

"Let's get down the mountain fast. Tires look fine. I'll pay for valet parking when we get to the hotel." Ed gave her another hug and nibbled her earlobe for a second. "Let's go, woman of mine."

Driving at the speed limit, they made it down the mountain into Reno just before snow began falling in earnest. Hillary followed Walt under the covered entrance to the Eldorado. Sarah got out and stretched, while the men unloaded their minimal luggage. The valet attendants drove the cars away.

The four of them entered the hotel's revolving door.

"So great to be here safe and sound," Ed said. He looked at Walt. "And before the buffet closes!" Walt patted his belly and grinned.

Ed led the way to the registration desk and they checked into their rooms, Hillary and Sarah in one and Ed and Walt on a different floor of the hotel tower, as planned.

They wandered the casino, assaulted by clanging bells and tunes from the slot machines. They were looking for the buffet, tucked away on purpose, thought Hillary, to offer plentiful chances to gamble.

Although hungry, Hillary couldn't resist stopping to slip change into slots blinking from every square foot of the vast expanse. She favored the old-fashioned machines with pull handles, so much more sensual than the push-button electronic kinds. Sarah kept her moving along, pointing at arrows leading to the buffet elevator.

After whisking up the tower, they reached the buffet entry, bristling with pine and holly berry garlands.

Hillary slipped her hand into Ed's. They stood at a huge glass window looking out at the wintery scene. As it feathered its way down, snow coated trees into fat white outlines. A living Christmas card, Hillary thought, inhaling the piney scent of the room, mixed with the aroma of the hotel's famous prime rib.

"Let's eat!" Hillary led the way from the viewpoint window to the maitre'd, glad the crowd had thinned out now at nearly ten o'clock. The prime rib glistened under the heat lamp.

"Shall we call this our rehearsal dinner?" She laughed. "Informally speaking."

Ed ordered a couple bottles of California red wines to go with the prime rib. Eating and drinking consumed the next hour and a half, until Walt signaled he'd had his fill.

Next up was the Wanda Sykes show, her zany comedy therapeutic after their harrowing drive in the sleety rain.

A couple hours after midnight, the women went up to their room, Hillary eager for the morning. Sarah made chamomile tea and served a cup to Hillary. They sat at the room's tiny table, Sarah in a print flannel nightgown. She braided her thick white hair into a single plait down the middle of her back. Then she braided Hillary's hair as well, and wrapped the coil around her head like a crown.

It was comforting to have Sarah with her, fussing over her. "What kind of mother were you?" Hillary asked. "When your kids were little."

"You'd need to ask Millie and Chris. But I tried to be calm and reasonable. Our people," she looked at Hillary with a serious face, "the Miwok-Maidu, we want to raise children to respect the earth, respect each other, and their parents and ancestors."

Hillary remembered how hostile Millie had been to her at the gathering after the burial of Sarah's husband. Millie was probably just trying to protect her good mother.

After she finished her tea, Hillary got into the queen bed on her side of the room. *What kind of mother will I be? My child could even turn out to be in line to run the Broome family business. Broome. Never know what's going to happen with Violet and Maggie. Tomorrow I'll be Hillary Kiffin instead of Broome. Should I use Ed's last name?*

Hillary fell into a restless sleep, dreaming of Monopoly houses and hotels, green and red plastic pieces tumbling from a night sky, tumbling down a mountainside covered with snow, tumbling and falling but never landing. Her own mother, so long absent, but grown tall in the dream, stood looking over the cold scene, paintbrush in one hand, palette in the other, scowling.

TWENTY-THREE

Hillary

HILLARY WAS ROLLING head over heels down the side of an icy mountain, growing fatter and fatter like a snowball. Waking with a start, she realized her covers had fallen to the floor. Yanking them back on, she dozed, exhausted from dreams, trying to keep them at bay.

Sarah's voice slid softly into her ear. "Rise and shine, Miss Bridey," she murmured. "Room service brought us a wake-up call."

Hillary smelled coffee and opened her eyes to see Sarah place a cup of dark brew on the nightstand, then set down a small silver pitcher of cream next to it.

No one had ever brought her coffee in bed. She sat

up and looked at the clock. It was only eight and they didn't have to meet the men for a couple more hours. "Thank you, Sarah. You're spoiling me. I bet Ed won't do this tomorrow morning!"

"You ask me, he just might," Sarah said. "That guy is crazy in love with you, Miss Bridey."

Hillary poured cream into her cup. She took her coffee to the window, drew open the drapes, and gasped. Sunshine cast a blinding light into the room. She picked up her coffee and took several big swallows, standing in the sunlight with her eyes closed, letting the caffeine work its magic.

From behind her, she could hear Sarah pouring herself coffee from the room service pot. "A good omen, the sunshine. I remember the song from the war years my mother's friends used to sing." Sarah started humming a tune, then belted out the words real loud: "Happy the bride the sun shines on today!"

Hillary listened, her eyes still closed. She savored her coffee and the delicious warmth of the room with Sarah in it, singing to her. Something entirely new.

"The song was about apple blossom time," Sarah said, "but it works whenever the sun is shining on a wedding day, you ask me." She refilled Hillary's cup. "We had the sunshine, John and I did. Yes, ma'am, Miss Bridey!"

It was wonderful to have Sarah here, like having a real mother in her life. Someday she should try to find her. Was she still somewhere in the South Pacific, Tahiti or Samoa or such? Was the sun perpetually shining in her tropical world?

Or should she just let that mother rest in peace? Be thankful for Sarah. So hard to know what to do with family. So much easier in the work world, getting the facts, getting the story, getting other people's stories. And ignoring her own.

* * *

At ten, Hillary and Sarah entered the hotel's breakfast cafe. Ed and Walt were already seated but rose when they saw the women coming toward them. Ed walked forward to embrace Hillary and hold her for a few long seconds. Walt pulled out a chair for Sarah.

After he seated Hillary, Ed poured coffee for the women from a large carafe, his eyes fastened on Hillary. "December 8th will be our anniversary." He looked like a man in love, his features arranged in a starstruck grin. Hillary took a mental photo of his face against the backdrop of the snow-white landscape shining through the window.

"Good thing we skipped Pearl Harbor Day—no bombings allowed, right?" She laughed and poured cream into her cup.

Ed frowned. "Let's eat, then get outdoors and look for the Justice of the Peace or a wedding chapel. No bombings at all," he said. Then his expression lightened. "The breakfast bar has corned beef hash." He winked at Hillary. "It won't be as good as yours, but . . ."

Hillary's heart felt young and joyful. She had made

the right decision.

"Let's go find what we're here for." She breathed fast. "Where did the concierge say to go? It's too cold to just wander around."

"There's a wedding chapel down the street," said Sarah, buttoning up her coat. "It's called Silver Bells or something like that. You two can get hitched and Walt and I can get over the mountains before the next storm decides to roll in."

"I'm ready!" Hillary led the way out the hotel's revolving doors into the bright and frigid air. "Put on your sunglasses, guys. Not a cloud in the sky."

"Yet." Walt slipped on his shades and pointed to his left. "Down that way."

The four of them tromped down the icy sidewalk. The long block was the shortest Hillary'd ever traveled. They were at the white picket fence of the wedding chapel and inside it before she realized what was happening. She had never thought of getting married in a place like this—a Justice of the Peace had seemed more respectable somehow. But then again, she'd never let herself picture much about a wedding at all.

An energetic middle-aged couple greeted them. "No need to make a separate trip for your license, dear hearts. We have the complete package!" The man looked pleased with himself and nodded at the woman by his side. "Albert and Helen at your service to handle everything."

Hillary was glad she'd not wasted time on getting new clothes. She was so cold from the walk outside, she hadn't even taken off her jacket. White candles flickered from wall sconces and added to the warmth of the room. It was nicer than she had expected.

Ed and Hillary signed some papers. Then Albert and Helen carried out a tray of flowers. The two men were outfitted with white carnation boutonnières, and Sarah a corsage of white roses. Hillary took off her jacket and stood with her gold silk blouse gleaming in the light from the candles. She reached out to take a bouquet of white roses surrounded by carnations. The flowers smelled fresh and spicy. Soft music filtered through the room's hush.

Hillary and Ed did as directed and stood in front of Albert. He had a book open on a lectern, decorated with white poinsettias.

"Dearly beloved," he began. Hillary almost let out a nervous laugh, but ducked her head and converted the impulse into drawing her gauzy scarf up over her head for the look of a veil. She hadn't expected this place to have a traditional ceremony, but Albert and his wife went through the basics of a generic Christian wedding service.

When Albert got to the ring part, Ed nodded at Walt, who pulled the wedding band from his pocket. Ed held it out toward Hillary's left hand, already fitted with his grandmother's antique diamond solitaire.

Hillary was dazzled by the new ring, a circle of gold with tiny emeralds in a row across the top.

He slipped the ring on with ease, pushing it up next to her diamond, his eyes smiling into hers, repeating Albert's words. "With this ring, I thee wed," he started out.

Hillary began to cry, her right hand clenched

around Ed's arm as he finished his lines and added, "The emeralds are for Ireland, someday."

After that, Albert said Ed could kiss the bride and when he did, sounds of "Congratulations" rang out. A cork popped. Helen poured pale bubbling wine into six glass flutes. Hillary's heart nearly skipped a beat when she heard the faint melody from Anne Murray's "You Needed Me." Now she felt strong enough for need.

At Albert's direction they all stood in front of the lectern, backgrounded by the wall of white candles. They raised their flutes in a toast, sipping and hugging, while the preset camera on the opposite wall took a dozen photos at 30-second intervals.

"No need to throw the bouquet today," Sarah quipped. "I won't be the next to get married and Helen, well, she's got Albert!" Everyone laughed. Sarah cupped Hillary's left hand in both of hers. "That is the most beautiful ring I ever saw."

They gathered up their things, and Ed handed Hillary her jacket. "Let's get out of here, Mrs. Kiffin." He hugged her. "We've got places to go."

Albert and Helen presented some papers in a white folder. "You can come back in a few hours to select your pictures," Helen said.

Walt pulled open the door. "Let's go to the celebration lunch! Come on!" He led the way out and back down the long block to the hotel casino, holding Sarah's arm when they got to the icy patches. Hillary and Ed walked as one person, arms locked—kissing, glancing at the sidewalk, kissing some more. More than once, one of them slipped but was caught by the other in time to prevent falling.

She closed her eyes and let this man she could trust lead her down the icy sidewalk. They turned into the revolving door. *I'm a married woman now.*

Walt was fifty feet ahead of them. The aisles were not yet crowded with gamblers so they could keep up with their best man, who was guiding Sarah along. They were headed to the elevator, on course for the roof's revolving restaurant.

"Let's get them a gift," Hillary whispered.

"Let's eat first," said Ed, "then slip out to the gift shop and get back before Walt finishes demolishing the dessert table. The one time I'm glad to count on his gluttony."

"Sounds like a plan," Hillary laughed. They were becoming a team. Now if they could just keep it up. What had gone wrong with her father and mother? She wished she knew the real story, so she could avoid their mistakes.

Hillary and Ed found their friends and sat down. At their table was a tiny wedding cake with a miniature bride and groom figure set on top. It looked so unlike them, but Hillary nearly started crying again.

"How darling! Did you get this?" she asked Sarah, who nodded and smiled. Hillary hugged Sarah. "What a surprise."

"Let's eat," boomed Walt, punching Ed in the arm and striding away toward a counter featuring King Crab legs, splayed out on a bed of ice.

The day was surpassing Hillary's notion of what it

should be. She was brimful of joy and didn't feel like eating. Ed stood near and slipped her jacket from her shoulders. He hung it over the back of her chair and then rubbed his hand over the pale gold silk of her collar. "Let's just get them a gift later, sit here and enjoy our little cake. What say?" He lifted her hand to his lips and kissed her ring finger.

Hillary smiled and nodded. If only she could stay forever in this splendid day. And the night to come.

TWENTY-FOUR

Violet

I GOT KAYLYN TO WORK on the party for Hillary and Ed. It would be perfect to hold in BC's newest clubhouse. Its Mediterranean style evoked warmth even in the middle of winter. No need for a formal sit down affair, a casual gathering would do just fine. There was a good-sized reception hall and a kitchen stocked with glass and china. Yellow roses would bring the flavor of summer into the affair even if the valley fog set in. After Kaylyn confirmed the date was good for most of the family, I leafed through Dad's Rolodex and picked out plenty of business contacts plus others from our community for Kaylyn to contact next.

At home after work, I was surprised to find Buddy hadn't returned from his medical conference. The house was empty.

In the silence, I wondered if I should give Maggie a chance to back off, leave me alone, let me run things. I picked up the phone. Her number was etched in my memory like everything else about her. No answer. After a minute, I hung up and redialed in case I'd punched in the wrong numbers. She'd never had an answering machine and I let it go to twenty rings before I gave up.

What was I going to say to the woman, anyway? Stay the hell out of my life? Don't think you can bring Dad's bastard son around and push him forward to shove me out?

I had to have faith. Caty's spell of protection was at the office, working its power to shield me. It was good I'd sprinkled some here, too.

Buddy would be home soon. I'd wait for him before I ate. I put some soup on the stove to simmer. Opening the mortgage loan spreadsheets on my laptop, I began going over the most current ones. The week after Dad died, when Teddy was in charge for that short time, we showed a different preferred lender. That was odd. Had Teddy wanted to stop working with Mortenson?

The phone rang.

"Sorry I haven't called sooner," said Buddy. "But I stopped by the emergency room on my way home. Wanted to look over the intake forms to see how they stack up against some new ideas from one of the conference panels."

"No problem," I said, getting up to stir the soup. "I've got tomato beef barley simmering for when you get here."

"The damnedest thing at the ER," Buddy said. "A young kid from over at a basketball game came in. Collapsed at halftime. They had me take a look at him, thought it might be asthma or such, but no."

"A basketball player?" It couldn't be related. I walked into the living room, phone in one hand, soup spoon in the other.

"Yeah, some student from Ford High. They just pronounced him dead. Name of Angel, so maybe he's on his way to heaven."

I froze. A couple drops of soup fell onto the carpet. "What?" *What did he say?*

"HCM, Hypertrophic Cardiomyopathy. It's not uncommon in teens. A heart condition undiscovered until the stress of athletics pushes the kid over the edge. Usually a young male." Buddy sighed. "Damn shame."

"Ummm . . ." Words stuck in my throat.

"Weird thing was that Maggie was there. Sitting with a Mexican woman who was crying her eyes out. Mother of the kid, I'm pretty sure. Sad."

I was speechless.

"I'll be home in a bit. Keep the soup hot. And the bed warm." Buddy laughed.

I hung up without a word. Caty's protection had gone beyond my wildest dreams. Angel was gone. No wonder there was no answer at Maggie's.

Would she get back on her adoption fantasy now?

TWENTY-FIVE

Violet

I REACHED OVER and turned on the light. Five thirty. Okay, not too early. Buddy was snoring. I sat up quietly in bed. Got to get this baby started before Maggie recovers from Angel's death and gets back to her screwy adoption idea.

The thermometer was in the highball glass I kept it handy in. It made a tinkling sound as I took it out and put it under my tongue. Maggie used to take my temperature rectally, jabbing it in and making me cry. What a mother. I needed to do a better job.

The thermometer registered in under a minute and I looked at it carefully. Yes. Finally. A significant drop. I was about to ovulate! Time to wake Buddy soon. I smiled, got up and took a shower. Then I put on a new nightgown, a winter Mrs. Santa style from Victoria's Secret. I climbed back under the covers, ready to give Buddy an early Christmas present. And get one in return.

We did it every which way but missionary, doggie being the recommended style for getting pregnant. Afterward, I lay inert, cells throbbing all over. Buddy got up and made coffee. The smells drifted down the hall to our room. I kept my eyes shut, visualizing all those little guy sperms swimming like mad to be the one. The one to pierce my big fat egg just starting to roll down the fallopian tube. Where would they meet and greet? A pang of unexpected sorrow shot through me. What about that little girl who would never have a chance. Is this how God loads the dice? How I turned out a girl and Ted a boy?

The sound of Buddy clearing his throat brought me back into the room.

"Coffee for madam," he said in his version of a French accent. Clearing a spot amid the thermometer supplies, he set a mug on the nightstand.

I reached out for another hug. Buddy plopped down on the side of the bed. We wrestled around, laughing.

"Come to mama," I crooned. The coffee grew cool in its mug. The morning moved slowly through us—it was good to be the boss and not have to be at the office on the dot of nine.

Later, Buddy got up and took the coffee mug back to the kitchen. I could hear him throwing out the potful grown cold by now and starting a new one. I got up and took another shower. The boy swimmers had had plenty of time to produce a winner. Now, if only Maggie let go of her threat to adopt. The woman was crazy. At her age. No agency would give her kids.

TWENTY-SIX

Hillary

WHEN HILLARY GOT HOME from Reno and heard about Angel, she called Violet right away. Hillary didn't feel she could mince words and got directly to the point, worried over how passionate Violet was about keeping control of BC.

"You didn't have anything to do with his death, did you?"

"Of course not. I wouldn't outright kill to keep the company," Violet screeched. "What do you think I am?"

"You can take Grandad's trust to court," Hillary said, " . . . break the male-first aspect. I would support you—we could all go, all us girl cousins, make it a sort of mini-class action suit."

"That's sweet of you, but . . ."

"I mean it. You don't need this much drama around getting to stay CEO."

"Well." Violet coughed. "Do you happen to know if Maggie will still try that crazy adoption scheme?"

"I'm going to call her now. She's not a woman who gives up without a fight."

Violet sighed. "You think I don't know that?"

"I'll get back to you if I learn anything," Hillary said. This family soup was getting thicker and thicker.

"Knowing her, she'll get it in high gear," Violet growled, then switched topics. "How did the Reno trip go? Are you Mrs. Kiffin now?"

Hillary laughed. "Yes, but I'm keeping the Broome name, just like you. After all, it was my father's and known in the news world, too. Not just the rich developers' world."

Violet laughed. "Having money comes in very handy at times, Hilly. For example, I've got all the reception arrangements made for you and Ed."

"You shouldn't have. I don't really have anybody to invite. Well, Sarah, maybe Walt and Roger. But Ed's family is back East—his only friends are other deputies." The truth was that Ed was entirely out of touch with his daughter as well as the rest of his family. Sarah, too, wasn't close to her children anymore. *We're all on the orphan side, looking to belong somewhere.*

"Not to worry, Hil." Violet was sounding much friendlier since Hillary'd warned her about Angel. "It'll be fun. An excuse to launch the new clubhouse—just family and a few close business associates."

Hillary got off the phone, her gut cramped with worry about the reception. She didn't want any Broome family drama ruining the start to her new life with Ed.

She rang up Maggie. It was Luisa who answered in a bare whisper. Hillary didn't know what to say to express condolences about her son. It was supposed to be a secret yet Hillary knew Luisa had heard her telling Maggie about the boy.

"This is Hillary, and I'm so sorry about the news," Hillary said. "I wonder if I may speak with Maggie?"

No answer. Hillary held on through a minute or two of silence. At least Luisa hadn't hung up the phone.

"Yes?" With just one word, Maggie's voice sounded as strong as ever.

"I wanted to express my condolences about Angel." Would Maggie hang up on her? Several seconds passed.

"Don't think this saves Violet, that pretender. You can tell your cousin I said so." After the click, a dial tone—loud and clear.

Hillary was stunned. What did she know about mother-daughter conflicts anyway? But she had to warn Violet.

TWENTY-SEVEN

Violet

AFTER CATY AGREED, I drove over and borrowed her book with the title that had branded itself in my mind: *Poisonous Plants*. I was on a mission since Hillary'd confirmed my insane mother was back on her adoption kick. I took the book home and snuggled up with it in bed.

Glancing through the table of contents, I was drawn to the chapter on belladonna. What a musical name.

Belladonna—beautiful lady in Italian. It was among the most lethal of herbal agents. I loved the irony. Maggie had so often pointed out her attractive appearance and advised me to stick to the ladylike pursuit of good looks, to keep my nose out of men's work. There was no sense waiting to hear if she was going to go through with her mean-spirited plan. I better solve this problem now. Get it off my plate.

Yes, belladonna. *Poisonous Plants* noted that all parts of the plant are loaded with atropine and scopolamine, the seeds being most potent. They had a side effect of atropine overdose.

Atropine overdose. I went into the bathroom and got the bottle from the medicine chest. The warnings on my prescription for menstrual cramps said the same thing. Can lead to tachycardia. Maggie's heart trouble had started soon after Teddy and I were born. She'd never made a secret of it. Blamed it on her not having more sons for our father.

I would be able to use the powder inside the capsules I'd been taking since my teens for my excruciating periods.

And here it was, right in my own house. This must be a sign, the right way to go. I held the bottle cradled in my hand and went back to read more. The genus name "atropa" comes from Atropos, one of the three Fates in Greek mythology—fates, yes. Mine and Maggie's. Bound together at the start and now here at the end. Bound together in the worst way like the fatal attraction of mortal enemies.

But the fates were finally with me. She'd brought me into the world. I'd help her out of it.

I went ahead and Googled "belladonna" to make extra sure. The main agent in belladonna was atropine with power to push heart rates way past normal. There was an antidote, but no one would have it at the party. It would look like Maggie's heart gave out. Everyone knew she'd been under Dr. Sloan's care for years.

I opened one of the capsules and sprinkled some into my palm. Licking my fingertip, I tapped the pale sandy powder to lift a speck to my tongue. It had practically no taste. Palm open, I took it back into the bathroom and, using the other hand, filled a glass with water. I brushed the powder into the water and watched it sink to the bottom. It just sat there, looking like a bit of pale grit at the bottom of the glass. But the bubbles in the reception champagne would stir it up.

Yes. Maggie was petite so it wouldn't take much. Triple the amount I used for my periods should do the job, I thought. I could carry the powder in my pill case. Dropping belladonna into her champagne would kill her. It would look like a natural death from heart failure. No need for an autopsy or tests for toxics.

Wait a minute. Didn't want her to collapse at the toast to the bride and groom, spoil the reception I'd worked to produce. Better wait until near the end. Cake and coffee. I'd seen her drink coffee at the lawyers. Coffee with cream. Shouldn't be that hard to drop powder into it. Give it a quick stir. The powder would dissolve better in the hot liquid anyway.

I smiled.

TWENTY-EIGHT

Hillary

HILLARY HAD RELISHED THE LUXURY of their wedding night and the king-sized bed with a mirror on the ceiling. Back at the cottage, she and Ed cuddled up close in her bed, more than cozy on these cold nights. His bachelor pad studio wasn't much better. They were going to have to get a bigger place, and soon.

She waited until Ed left for work before she called Violet. It was a surprise when Buddy answered.

"Hey, how are you?" she asked. *Should I tell him what I'm worried about?*

"Sleepy, how about you?"

"A beaming bride." She laughed. "Is Violet home?"

"Ms. CEO took off early today. Wanted to get everything ready for your reception."

"That's really nice of her." Hillary cleared her throat. "I'm a tiny bit concerned though, Buddy."

"About what?"

"I'm just praying that Violet can get over her anger at Maggie, you know? I wouldn't want her to do anything she'd regret later."

"Like what?" Buddy's voice took on a somber tone.

"Well, you know, Maggie keeps working on shoving Violet out of BC. I'm trying to convince Vi she should take the trust to court, but she doesn't seem interested."

"Really?" His voice was cool.

"I'm worried Vi might be planning to, well, do something drastic to Maggie. I might be going overboard on this, but just wanted to run it by you."

"You barely know her, Hillary. Seems unwarranted for you to suspect your cousin of harming her own mother."

"I'm sorry, Buddy. I shouldn't have brought it up. Please don't mention I said anything to Violet."

"I have faith in her and most definitely won't communicate your misplaced concern." He hung up without saying good-bye.

Hillary felt sweaty. But when she was honest with herself, she imagined her elation at getting revenge on her own mother. And Violet hadn't been far away when both Teddy and Angel died.

Maybe her warning to Buddy would do some good.

TWENTY-NINE

Hillary

ON THE WAY TO THE RECEPTION, Hillary was excited and worried at the same time. She glanced at Ed, his face straight ahead, eyes on the road. It was wonderful to feel so secure with him now. She pushed a CD into the slot. Anne Murray's golden tones started up. "Could I Have this Dance." *For the rest of my life.* She'd told Violet this was the music she wanted for their first dance at the reception. The song moved her to the verge of tears.

She turned to study Ed's profile. He looked handsome in his wedding suit, competent, in the driver's seat, but his brows were knit. "What's that frowny face?" She tapped him a couple times on the cheek.

He laughed. "Sorry, Chickadee. Just on guard when we're going to a Broome occasion."

Hillary sighed. She twisted her rings around on her finger, too nervous to relax and enjoy being the bride. She prayed Maggie wouldn't even show up. "I hope everything goes smoothly." She ran her hands over the nubby fabric of the brown and gold outfit she'd worn in Reno. Not a white gown, but special to her now. She wouldn't put the scarf over her head like a veil this time, though.

"Tule fog moving in tonight," Ed said. "Damn nice of Violet to throw this for us. What are you concerned about?" Ed took the ramp for the short drive north on I-5.

"Violet has become obsessed over being in charge at BC. She has to have it all her way. I have a hunch she's planning something to stop Maggie."

"I'll keep an eye out." Ed turned off the freeway and headed for the reception, a mile down the road.

As they approached through swirling patches of fog, Hillary admired the clubhouse, looking like it came off an *Architectural Digest* cover. Silvery icicles hung from the rooflines, topped by sparkling snowflakes in all sizes and shapes. Ed pulled into the parking space sign-marked for them, and they made their way to the portico. Hillary was glad to see Roger at the sidelines snapping photos as they arrived.

Wearing a splashy purple jacket over black pants, Violet greeted them with open arms and hugs. "Nice outfit," Hillary said, running her hands over Violet's velvet jacket and nodding down at her silky dress pants.

"Love yours, too." Violet fluffed up Hillary's fancy scarf and gave her a kiss on the cheek.

By Violet's side stood Buddy, the ever-faithful husband. He shook hands with Ed and nodded at Hillary. *He's got a grudge against me now. Shouldn't have warned him.*

From out of the creeping tule fog, a black limo pulled up at the entrance and out stepped Maggie, dressed in a peacock-patterned coat. She turned back to smile at two teenaged boys as they got out of the limo, dressed in tailored suits a bit too long in the sleeves for them.

Hillary was shocked and watched to see how Violet would react. She simply smiled toward Maggie and vanished through the tall doors, as if to lead the way into the party. *How can Violet hide her feelings like that? I know she'd like to kill the witch.*

Hillary took Ed's hand and they followed Violet inside. A string quartet was playing soft classical music, setting a serene tone over the open space, beginning to fill with chattering guests.

And there was Walt, puffed up with pride as if he'd created the newlywed pair. *That's what Dad would have looked like.* Hillary blinked back tears. Nearby stood Sarah, beaming her down-to-earth smile. Hillary's heart warmed to the celebration. *Family and friends. I do have some after all.*

Violet lined Ed and Hillary up not far from the front doors, with Sarah and Walt next to them. Her assistant

Kaylyn pinned on corsages for the women and boutonnières for the men. Violet waved over several people to
get the receiving line started.

Jake Mortenson grabbed Ed's hand. "A pleasure to
meet you. I'm hoping you and your beautiful bride will
be house shopping soon?" He winked at Hillary and gave
her a hug. "You two let me know if you need any special
help."

Hillary swallowed and nodded but before she could
think of a good comeback, Ed was shaking hands with a
woman and introducing her to Hillary as Donna, the
Broome Construction interior designer.

"Teddy would have loved this," the blonde waved
her hands towards the walls. "Byron and I," she nodded
toward a young man with spiky black hair and pierced
about the eyebrows and lips. "we know Teddy appreci-
ated our work to create this room for happy times like
. . ." Her voice caught in her throat. Hillary hugged her
gently. *Let's just pray we don't have any tragedies at* this
family party.

As others moved through the line, Ed agreed how
lucky he was and talked about a honeymoon next summer. Hillary showed off her rings and introduced guests
to Sarah and Walt. Flanked by her new husband and her
stand-in mother, Hillary glowed with a sense of belonging.

* * *

During a brief lull, Hillary searched the room to see how close Violet was to Maggie but lost track of them both. She spotted Walt as he slipped over to a nearby hors d'oeuvres table, picked up a toast square oozing with melted cheese, and popped it into his mouth. She caught Ed's eye and tossed her head in Walt's direction. He shook his head and grinned as Walt adroitly stepped back in line next to Sarah, his mouth closed as he chewed.

* * *

As she shook hands, smiling and hugging, Hillary kept an eye out for Maggie. She was all over the room, guiding the boys around, introducing them to family and business associates. How would Violet take this grab for power? Hillary's blood felt heavy in her veins.

Within a few minutes, her black eyes sparkling, Maggie approached the receiving line. "Darlings," she said, "so happy for you. Have you met Frank and Victor? Identical twins. Orphaned by a catastrophic house fire, poor kids. They'll be inheriting all this soon." Maggie stretched both arms out in a gesture suggesting more than the clubhouse. She looked up at the teens, tall and handsome in a young George Clooney sort of way. The boys stared down at the floor, expressionless. "Now, don't be shy."

Maggie turned to Hillary. "They need a little polish." She leaned near the one closest to her. "Victor, shake hands with your soon-to-be cousin Hillary," she said in a stage whisper.

Hillary reached out for the young man's hand. Suddenly, he bowed, grasped her fingers and kissed her hand. "Pleased ta meetcha," he said in some kind of accent.

Maggie laughed. "Victor can be so entertaining. Has the gift of gab like my darling husband did."

Hillary smiled. *Poor kid. He doesn't have a clue what this family's like. Where is Violet? She must be freaked out over Maggie's public display of these boys.*

Their receiving line duties complete, Ed and Hillary mingled among the guests. A couple of men stood behind a bar pouring a selection of wines. On a nearby table, a mound of wedding gifts seemed to be growing by the minute. Hillary stopped to admire an ice sculpture of two doves, wingtip to wingtip. Nearby was a stunning wedding cake, yellow roses spiraling down its sides. An ornate silver cake knife was positioned in front of the cake.

Violet might try to stab Maggie with that knife. But then she almost laughed out loud.

That's ridiculous!

The string quartet started up a dreamy waltz. Violet stepped up to a microphone at the edge of the dance floor outlined on the parquet flooring. Her voice rang out: "Ladies and Gentlemen, I'm pleased to present to you, Mr. and Mrs. Ed Kiffin." She gave a nod in Hillary's direction as the crowd applauded and the music swelled. Hand in hand, Ed and Hillary stepped onto the dance floor as the guests moved back to clear space.

Cheek to cheek with this man who needed her, Hillary's body swirled in rhythm with Ed's limber grace. It was the first time they'd danced. She lost track of Violet and Maggie and gave herself to the moment. "For the rest of our life," Ed whispered, as the strings quivered with this melody for lovers.

Walt tapped Ed on the shoulder for his turn to dance with the bride. She watched as Ed took Sarah's hand. Her face as they waltzed gave a picture of Sarah as a young woman.

Walt was light on his feet for such a heavy man. Hillary hoped Roger was getting plenty of casual shots. As others joined in the waltz, Hillary tried to spot Violet and Buddy on the dance floor, but Violet was nowhere to be seen. *Where is she?*

The music faded. Servers moved through the large hall, offering flutes of champagne from trays.

Out of nowhere, Violet was at the mic again. "Please help yourselves to our sparkling California champagne. The best man, Ed's partner in crime," she paused for a laugh from the guests, "will toast the newlyweds first." She nodded in Walt's direction and walked away from the mic. Hillary spied her patting her pants pockets. *What could she have hidden there?*

Walt lumbered over to the mic, waving a three-by-five card. "Need notes, folks." He cleared his throat and adjusted his necktie. "Some of you might know, I'm not the biggest fan," he waited a beat, "of marriage. In general, that is." He pointed to Ed, standing nearby. "But this guy," Walt looked at his notecard, "this guy's someone I want to see in a good mood. That's because I have to spend every blasted working day at his side. And let me tell you, after he gave up smoking cigars but before this young lady came along," he nodded at Hillary, "this guy was at me so much of the time," he glanced at his notecard, "about health and fitness and eating right, that one day I kept count." Walt waved the card in the air. "Kept tally marks every time this know-it-all pointed out to me what I needed to do. And on that day," Walt cleared his throat, "Ed told me seventeen times, seventeen in one day, how I needed to improve myself. Thanks, Hillary," he raised his glass, "for taking Ed's mind off of me!"

Guests laughed and clapped as Walt took a swallow of champagne and walked over to punch the red-faced Ed in the arm and give Hillary a kiss on the cheek.

Violet returned to the mic. "Sarah, your turn, you Wonder Woman—matron of honor and mother of the bride all in one."

Sarah stepped up to the mic. "Just want to wish these young people the years of happiness my John and I had together—miss him every day. So make sure to stop and smell the roses, both of you." She turned her head to brush her cheek against her corsage. "Yellow roses symbolize friendship, delight, and the promise of a new beginning." She raised her glass high in Hillary's direction.

Hillary had lost track of Violet again. Where could she be disappearing to?

Amid the clapping, Hillary and Ed walked to the mic. "Thank you all for showing up to cheer us on." Ed looked around the room. "We didn't know we had so many friends, did we, Chickadee?" Hillary blushed a deep crimson. He had hit her most vulnerable place—belonging. She didn't say a word, just nodded with a bright face.

She had to get out of there for a minute, go splash cold water on her face. She pushed open the ladies room door and gasped. Violet was shoving something into the pocket of her silky black pants. "What are you doing?"

"Just tucking in a tissue in case my hands get sweaty when we do the cake next. You are such a beautiful bride and friend to me." Violet opened her arms and gave Hillary a warm hug. Hillary backed away and held Violet at arms length.

"How can you look so friendly, with Maggie flaunting those boys?

"I've been working with a sort of therapist woman, trying to get help in managing my challenges." Violet flashed a brilliant smile and waltzed out. The cold water cooled off Hillary's face but not her suspicions.

Violet appeared with a proud smile to announce the cutting of the cake. She wiped her palms and then handed Hillary the traditional Broome silver cake knife. Hillary knew what her cousin would love to do with that knife if only she could get away with it. Yet, Violet's face remained serenely joyous.

Roger was busy taking photos as they cut into the cake and made their wedding wishes. They got the first pieces, vanilla with a lemon filling—a perfect match to the yellow roses spiraling down the sides. Servers carried trays of cake and coffee around to the guests.

Hillary lost track of Violet in the swirl of bodies. She

and Ed set their cake on one of the tables scattered around the room. She took a bite from the middle, the lemon filling. She nodded with pleasure as Ed did the same.

At the next table, Violet appeared, smiling at Maggie, sitting there with cake for herself and the twin boys. Violet turned to a nearby server and took a couple cups of punch to hand to the boys. They downed the punch like parched survivors in a desert.

Maggie nodded as Violet handed her a cup of coffee in one hand and a pitcher of cream in the other. Maggie reached out for them and set them on the table. She poured cream into her coffee and looked away to watch Victor who was pantomiming Charlie Chaplin, stiff-walking down an imaginary aisle toward Frank, standing a few feet away with hands clasped as if a bride holding a bouquet. Maggie clapped and nodded at others enjoying the show.

Hillary spotted Violet's hand hovering over her mother's cup.

Her hand opened and a spoon appeared as if by magic. It dipped into the cup. Violet stirred in tiny circles. Then she backed away.

Holy Mary. Hillary muttered to Ed to stay alert before she rushed over to Buddy. She hissed that he better go grab Maggie's coffee. Buddy glared at Hillary with ice blue eyes. "You've got my wife all wrong. You must be jealous." He did nothing.

Hillary felt paralyzed. She watched Maggie turn back to take a bite of wedding cake and chew for a few seconds before she set her fork down.

The drama playing out in front of Hillary's eyes struck her as impossible. This was her wedding reception. Was she going to have to transform it into a slow motion crime scene?

As Maggie lifted the coffee to her lips, Hillary bounded to her side and knocked the cup away, sending it flying six feet through the air and crashing to the floor. The china shattered and creamy coffee spread in a wide circle, pooling toward Maggie's feet.

Maggie jumped up, her mouth agape. Guests close by turned to see what the fuss was.

Violet was nearing the front doors.

"Ed!" screamed Hillary. "Stop her!"

Ed ran after Violet. Hillary followed, threading her way though wedding guests. Once outside, she lost sight of them in the thick tule fog. She could hear Violet screaming. "She . . . deserved it! Her heart . . . no good!"

Hillary turned in the direction of the sounds. Within seconds, she spotted them near Ed's unmarked.

"She's poison!" Ed held Violet immobile, her arms pinned. Violet's neck was wrenched around toward Ed. "She was trying to kill—"

Hillary ran to take Violet in her arms.

"You ruined it!" Violet kicked at Hillary's shins. "No one else saw." Violet kicked up at Hillary's belly. "You're no friend, no cousin of mine!"

"I couldn't let you," Hillary cried. "It would have been worse for you than for her, Vi."

Buddy rushed in through the fog, and Ed released

Violet into his arms.

"She was trying to kill me, Buddy!" Violet sobbed. "It was self defense, you know that, don't you?" She yammered those words over and over. Her mother was trying to kill her. It was self-defense.

Hillary stood cold and motionless, as if she were a dove carved out of ice at someone else's wedding, and couldn't fly away.

* * *

Hillary's fear had come true. Violet had tried to kill her mother. But it was better for her cousin to be up on charges of attempted murder than murder itself, wasn't it? Trying to murder your mother, witchy as she was— imagine that. Hillary tried to picture her own mother, so far away. A new feeling of gratitude slipped over her shoulders. She'd never thought she'd be glad that the woman was already dead to her.

Now, though, she might be dead to the Broome family.

THIRTY

Hillary

THE NEXT MORNING, Ed and Hillary drove through the fog over to the county jail compound south of Stockton.

"I can't believe it." Hillary blew her nose and coughed.

"At least we got her into the Psych Ward. It sure as hell isn't as bad as the regular jail." He cracked his neck.

"Psych Clinic. Never heard of anyone else in the family going over the top like that." Hillary sighed. "Not in a criminal way." She sat silent for long minutes. "Well, I don't know them as well as I'd like to." Her heart felt heavy. "I should have done more. I saw it coming but

Buddy didn't believe me."

Her arms ached with a cold emptiness. Violet. What would happen to her? Locked up.

* * *

They entered the bleak gray foyer of the Psych Ward. Hillary spotted a phone and lifted the receiver.

"We're here to see Violet. Violet Broome."

Hillary listened a few seconds then put the receiver back in its cradle. "The nurse is sending Buddy out to talk to us." She shuddered. "He probably wants to kill me."

"Jesus H. Christ, Hill!" Ed stood rigid in his bad cop stance and spoke through clenched teeth. "Give yourself credit. You saved her from being a murderer. He ought to be grateful as hell."

"Maybe she would have gotten away with it." Hillary shook her head and wished there was someplace to sit in the small gray lobby. "Maggie has a bad heart you know."

Buddy came bursting through the double doors into the foyer. He reached out with widespread arms and crushed Hillary against his chest. She stood frozen in place, holding her breath. She could feel him shaking. Was he trying to smother her?

She had to push against his chest to get room enough to gulp in some air. His pale blue eyes were streaming with tears.

"Thank you, thank you, thank you," he whispered.

Hillary felt numb. "For what?" she breathed.

"You saved Violet from reaching the bottom. With help, we can get her off. It's clear she's unable to stand trial for this."

"Does she hate me?"

"She's not in her right mind. You did the right thing—she will figure that out in time. I just hope she's not pregnant." He shuddered. "I've got to get back to her, but I'm sorry I ignored your warnings." He phoned for permission to get back through the locked doors and vanished into the ward.

* * *

Ed drove them over to Little Joe's. They sat in Hillary's favorite booth. Ed ordered a breakfast burrito and coffee but Hillary could only stomach a cup of tea.

"Violet is in the psych clinic because of her confession," Ed stirred his coffee, "so toxicology is not essential on the spilled coffee, but it'll be interesting to look at Roger's pictures. See if he got a shot of Vi dumping in the poison. And tox will show us what she used."

"I'd feel better if I saw that," Hillary nodded. "I was just acting on my suspicions."

"Ted's tox panels have finally come back and show that Ted's death was a natural allergic reaction to a combination of paprika and hazelnut," Ed explained, "but not so much in his system that it was suspected of being deliberate, according to the Medical Examiner's office.

"So Violet is off the hook on that count, anyway."

Ed turned to Joe and ordered fish tacos and Hillary murmured she'd have the same.

"Have to follow up still, wrap up looking into the
three stooges," he chuckled, "those other suspects—the
banker, Donna, and that crazy Mold Man. Probably
guilty of something but not killing Ted."

Hillary shook her head and sucked in her cheeks,
then blew out a long exhale. "*Holy Mary*. What a story
this is—stranger than fiction! I hope the family doesn't
shut me out for getting Violet put away behind bars."

"You could consider getting exiled from this family
a blessing." He laughed. "Just kidding. I know you love
them, crazy as they are."

Later that afternoon, while she was at *The Acorn*
writing up her account of the events, Roger put the photos up on his computer screen and showed her the picture he'd gotten of powder spilling from Violet's palm
into Maggie's cup. "That was a lucky shot, Dopey. And
you want to belong to that family?" He chuckled. Her
face burned. But it was true.

* * *

That night, Hillary got a call from cousin Joanna.
Hillary'd been worried she would be ostracized, but she
and Ed were invited to Joanna and Milan's for Christmas
dinner out at their place on the river. Joanna said she was
going to stick to the tried and true old family recipes and
not try anything new for awhile.

She told Hillary that because she was moving along

at high speed with her restaurant, Milan was going to take over as CEO of Broome Construction, running it for her since Violet was clearly no longer of sound mind, and she was the next cousin in line to inherit. Maggie said she was okay with that since Milan was a man—with a capable business sense. Joanna laughed. "Can you believe that woman!"

Hillary felt confident no judge would let Maggie adopt anyway, after this outrageous uproar. Grandad's conviction that men should be in charge seemed almost confirmed by Violet's actions, thought Hillary. She wanted the Broome family business to keep flourishing. It felt like part of her long-lost heritage. *I want to learn more about this Grandad, our Irish ancestor.*

* * *

On Christmas afternoon, Ed drove past Potato Slough along the Delta levee road toward Joanna and Milan's. "Potato Slough. Remember you cooked your soothing potato soup just a month ago at Thanksgiving?"

"Of course," Hillary said. "Then we were all recovering from Sarah nearly getting killed. Now we're adjusting to having a killer in the family. Too much horrific stuff happening around here. Let's go on a honeymoon, somewhere safe where I don't keep running into trouble. Maybe Ireland?" She ran her fingers through her long hair and smiled at her new husband, feeling giddy and happily ever after. For now.

THE END

ACKNOWLEDGMENTS

I'm grateful to Nanowrimo, National Novel Writing Month each November, during which I got House of Dads started in 2012. For support from then on, I appreciate my readers and cheerleaders: sisters Jacki and Jan; children Julie, Karen, and Mike; and friends Kay, Nancy and Leslie. Writing conferences and groups have been vital, as well, including Sisters in Crime, Capitol Crimes Sacramento Chapter—especially Michele, Pam, Linda and Mertianna. Auburn's Gold Rush Writers have offered enthusiastic encouragement and friendship, too, at our weekly meetings in the downtown Placer Arts Gallery.

Just as for House of Cuts, first in the Hillary Broome series, I'm grateful for the inspiration of Donna Tartt,

Jeff Lindsey, Thomas Harris, and Dean Koontz for their literary forays into so many rooms in the Psyche. For the seed idea of House of Dads, but not the actual story, I am indebted to my father, who years ago said no when asked if I could learn his painting contracting business. A yes would have aborted this novel. That's what's so wonderful about being a writer—we can turn all the disappointments into stories!

ABOUT THE AUTHOR

A native of California, June Gillam focuses on issues that bridge the light and the darkness of this journey we call life. Her poems have been published in regional outlets, with her first poetry collection, So Sweet Against Your Teeth, now in print. After she realized many of her poems wanted to be stories, she began writing short fiction and is published in venues such as *Metal Scratches* and *America's Intercultural Magazine*.

Now she's writing a series of novels featuring Hillary Broome, a redheaded reporter by trade who keeps falling into troublesome and life-threatening situations. Her novels have been compared to those of Jeffrey Lindsey's Dexter series and Jodi Picault's books focusing attention on current issues in the culture.

Visit the author at her website:
www.junegillam.com.

WHAT'S NEXT
for Hillary Broome?

On a trip to Ireland, Hillary is shocked to find her friend Bridget has been murdered on the Long Walk near Galway Bay. Hillary becomes embroiled in chasing down the killer, who's taunting the law by sending preposterous stories to the newspapers and laying the crime onto several infamous Irish ghosts, said to terrorize at night. Evidence mounts of a "Cover-up Killing" to shush news Bridget had uncovered, news that could quash an Irish theme park that's still but a developer's dream. In order to save innocent lives, Hillary must bring to light secrets buried as far back as the Irish Potato Famine and as recently as the 1990's Celtic Tiger, the sudden and fleeting growth of the Irish economy.

12347533R00148

Made in the USA
San Bernardino, CA
14 June 2014